Y0-AGI-440

"MR. POLK," SAID RANDY, "IT WAS NOT MY FAULT, AND I SHALL NOT STAND FOR THE DAMAGE DONE."—P. 223.

Randy of the River—Frontispiece

RANDY OF THE RIVER

OR

THE ADVENTURES OF A YOUNG DECKHAND

BY

HORATIO ALGER, JR.

AUTHOR OF "NELSON THE NEWSBOY," "OUT FOR BUSINESS,"
"THE YOUNG BOOK AGENT," "LOST AT SEA,"
"RAGGED DICK SERIES," ETC.

GROSSET & DUNLAP

PUBLISHERS :: :: NEW YORK

THE RISE IN LIFE SERIES

By Horatio Alger, Jr.

OUT FOR BUSINESS;
Or, Robert Frost's Strange Career.

FALLING IN WITH FORTUNE;
Or, The Experiences of a Young Secretary

NELSON THE NEWSBOY;
Or, Afloat in New York.

JERRY THE BACKWOODS BOY;
Or, The Parkhurst Treasure.

FROM FARM TO FORTUNE;
Or, Nat Nason's Strange Experience.

YOUNG CAPTAIN JACK;
Or, The Son of a Soldier.

THE YOUNG BOOK AGENT,
Or, Frank Hardy's Road to Success.

LOST AT SEA;
Or, Robert Roscoe's Strange Cruise

RANDY OF THE RIVER,
Or, The Adventures of a Young Deckhand.

Cloth. 12mo. Illustrated. Price, 60 cents per volume.

Randy of the River.

PREFACE

THE majority of stories for boys have their background laid either in the city or the country, or possibly on the ocean, and we have read much about the doings of lads both rich and poor in such locations.

In the present tale we have a youth of sturdy qualities who elects to follow the calling of a deckhand on a Hudson River steamboat, doing his duty faithfully day by day, and trying to help others as well as himself. Like all other boys he is at times tempted to do wrong, but he has a heart of gold even though it is hidden by a somewhat ragged outer garment, and in the end proves the truth of that old saying that it pays to be honest,—not only in regard to others but also regarding one's self.

Life on a river steamboat is not so romantic as some young people may imagine. There is hard work and plenty of it, and the remuneration is not of the best. But Randy Thompson wanted work and took what was offered. His success in the end was well deserved, and perhaps the lesson his doings teach will not be lost upon those who peruse these pages. It is better to do what one finds to do than to fold your hands and remain idle, and the idle boy is sure, sooner or later, to get into serious mischief.

CONTENTS

CONTENTS

RANDY OF THE RIVER

CHAPTER I

SOMETHING ABOUT RANDY

"I AM going fishing, Randy. Do you want to go along?"

"With pleasure, Jack," answered Randy Thompson, a bright, manly youth of fourteen. "Are you going on foot or in your boat?"

"I think we might as well take the boat," returned Jack Bartlett, a boy who was but a few months older than Randy. "Have you your lines handy?"

"No, but I can get them in less than ten minutes."

"All right. Meet me at the dock in quarter of an hour. I was thinking of going up the river to Landy's Hole. That's a good spot, isn't it?"

"I think so. Last season I was up there and caught fourteen good-sized fish."

"They tell me you are one of the best fishermen

in Riverport, Randy," went on Jack Bartlett, admiringly. "What is the secret of your success?"

"I don't know unless it is patience," answered Randy, with a broad smile. "To catch fish you must be patient. Now when I caught my mess of fourteen two other boys were up to the Hole. But just because the fish did not bite right away they moved away, further up the river. But by doing that they got only about half as many as myself."

"Well, I am willing to be patient if I know I am going to catch something."

At this Randy laughed outright.

"You can't be sure of anything—in fishing. But I always reckon it's a good thing to hold on and give a thing a fair trial."

"I reckon you're right, Randy, and I'll give the fishing a fair trial to-day," answered Jack Bartlett. "Remember, the dock in quarter of an hour," he added, as he moved away.

"I'll be on hand—unless mother wants me to do something for her before I go away," returned Randy.

Randy, or rather Randolph, Thompson, to use his right name, was the only son of Louis Thompson, a carpenter of Riverport, a thriving town in one of our eastern states. Randy had no brothers or sisters, and lived with his father and mother in a modest cottage on one of the side roads leading to the hills back of the town. Randy was a scholar in the local school, standing close to the head of his class. It was now summer time and the institution of learning was closed, so the boy had most of his time to himself.

He had wanted to go to work, to help his father, who had some heavy doctors' bills to pay, but his parents had told him to take at least two weeks' vacation before looking for employment.

"He needs it," Mrs. Thompson had said to her husband. "He has applied himself very closely to his studies ever since last fall."

"Well, let him take the vacation and welcome," answered Louis Thompson. "I know when I was a boy I loved a vacation." He was a kind-hearted man and thought a good deal of his offspring and also of his wife, who was devoted to him.

The cottage stood back in the center of a well-kept garden, where Mrs. Thompson had spent much time over her flowers, of which she was passionately fond. It was a two-story affair, containing but five rooms, yet it was large enough for the family, and Randy, who had never known anything better, considered it a very good home.

There was a small white fence in front, with a gate, and the path to the front stoop was lined with geraniums. Over the porch was trained a honeysuckle which filled the air with its delicate fragrance.

"Mother, I'm going fishing with Jack Bartlett!" cried Randy, running around to the kitchen, where his mother was busy finishing up the week's ironing.

"Very well, Randy," she answered, setting down her flatiron and giving him a smile. "I suppose you won't be back until supper time."

"It's not likely. Can I do anything for you before I go?"

"You might get a bucket of water and another armful of wood."

"I'll do that," answered Randy, and caught up the water bucket. "Anything else?"

"No. Take care of yourself while you are on the river."

"Don't worry about me, mother. Remember, I can swim like a fish."

"Yes, I know. But you must be careful anyway," answered Mrs. Thompson, fondly.

The water and wood were quickly brought into the cottage, Randy whistling merrily while he performed these chores. Then the youth ran for his fishing outfit, after which he took the spade, went down to the end of the garden, and turned up some worms, which he placed in a pasteboard box.

"Now I am off, mother!" he called out.

"Good-by, Randy," she said, and waved him a pleasant adieu from the open kitchen window.

"She's the best mother a boy ever had," thought Randy, as he walked away to join Jack at the dock.

"What a good boy!" murmured Mrs. Thompson. "Oh, I hope he grows up to be a good man!"

When Randy arrived at the dock he found himself alone. He brought out the boat and cleaned it up and got the oars. He was all ready for the start when a boy somewhat older than himself slouched up.

The newcomer was loudly dressed in a checked suit and wore a heavy watchchain, a big seal ring, and a diamond shirt stud. He might have been good-looking had it not been for the supercilious scowl of independence upon his face.

"Hullo there, Randy Thompson!" he called out. "What are you doing in Jack Bartlett's boat?"

His manner was decidedly offensive and did not suit Randy at all.

"I don't know as that is any of your business, Bob Bangs," he answered coldly.

"Humph! Jack won't thank you for getting out his boat," went on Bob Bangs. "If you want a boat why don't you hire one?"

"I don't have to hire one," answered Randy.

"You wouldn't dare to touch my boat," continued Bob, who was known as the town bully. His father was rich and for that reason he thought he could ride over all the other boys.

"I shouldn't care to touch it," said Randy.

"Don't you know you haven't any right to touch Jack's boat without his permission?" went on the big youth.

"Bob Bangs, this is none of your business."

"Humph! I'll make it my business."

"If you do, you may get into trouble."

"I'll risk that. If you don't get out of that boat I'll tell Jack."

"I am not going to get out of the boat."

"Maybe I'll make you get out," and Bob Bangs came a step closer, and put his hand on the gunwale of the rowboat.

"You leave me and the boat alone," said Randy, sharply.

"You get out of that boat."

"Not for you."

Bob Bangs looked ugly. He was on the point of catching Randy by the collar when an interruption came from behind.

"So you got here ahead of me, eh?" came in Jack's voice, as he approached on a swift walk. "I had to do an errand for father and that kept me."

As Jack came up Bob Bangs fell back in disgust.

"Humph! Why didn't you say you were waiting for Jack?" he said to Randy, with a sour look on his face.

"You didn't ask me, that's why," returned Randy.

"What's the trouble?" questioned Jack, quickly.

"Bob wanted me to leave the boat alone."

"I thought he was trying to sneak it on the sly," explained the big boy. "I didn't know you cared to go out with him," he added, to Jack, with a toss of his head.

"Why shouldn't I go out with Randy?" asked Jack, quickly.

"Oh, I shouldn't care to go out with the son of a poor carpenter."

"See here, Bob Bangs, I consider myself as good as you," said Randy, quickly.

"Humph!"

"Randy is all right, even if his father is a carpenter," said Jack. "It's mean of you, Bob, to talk that way."

"Choose your own company and I'll choose mine," answered Bob Bangs, loftily, and stalked away, his nose tilted high in the air.

Angry words arose to Randy's lips but he repressed them and said nothing. In a moment more some goods on the dock hid the big boy from view.

"Don't you care for what he says," said Jack, quickly. "He thinks a few dollars are everything in this world."

"I didn't mind him—much, Jack."

"Wanted you to get out of my boat, didn't he?"

"Yes. He didn't know I was waiting for you."

"That was a good joke on him."

"I can't understand why he is so disagreeable."

"It was born in him," said Jack, as he leaped into the rowboat and stowed away his fishing outfit. "His father is the same way and so is his mother. They think that just because they have money everybody else, especially a poor person, is dirt under their feet."

"Why, Jack, I guess your father is as rich as Mr. Bangs."

"Maybe he is."

"And you don't put on such airs."

"And I don't intend to. Money is a good thing to have, but it isn't everything—that is what my father and mother say."

"Bob wouldn't want me out in his boat with him."

"Maybe you wouldn't like to go out with him either."

"You are right there. I am getting so I hate to speak to him."

"Well, I am getting that way, too. Every time we meet he tries to impress it upon me that he is a superior person,—and I don't see it."

"Your father and his father have some business dealings, haven't they?"

"Yes, they are interested in the same iron company,—and from what father says, I think they are going to have trouble before long."

"I hope your father comes out ahead."

"It is this way: Father has a controlling interest and Mr. Bangs is doing his best to get it away from him. If Mr. Bangs can get control he will, so father says, join the company of a larger concern, and then father will be about wiped out and he won't get more than half of what is really coming to him."

"But wouldn't that be fraud?"

"Yes, morally, but not legally—so father says," answered Jack, and heaved a sigh. "I hope it all comes out right."

"And so do I—for your sake as well as for your folks," added Randy, heartily.

CHAPTER II

AT THE FISHING HOLE

THE fishing hole for which the two boys were bound was on the river about a mile and a half above the town. At this point the stream was thirty to forty feet wide and ten to fifteen feet deep. It was lined on one side with sharp rocks and on the other by thick trees and bushes. At the foot of some of the rocks, where the river made a bend, there was a deep hole, and this some of the lads, including Randy and Jack, considered an ideal place for fishing.

The boys did not row directly for the hole, being afraid they might scare the fish away. Instead they landed below the spot, tied fast to a tree root between the stones, and then crawled over the big rocks until they reached a point from which they could cast into the hole with ease.

They soon baited up. Randy was ready first, but he gave his companion the chance to make the initial cast. Scarcely had Jack's hook touched the water when there came a jerk and the line was almost pulled from the boy's hands.

"You've got him!" cried Randy, excitedly. "Good for you!"

"If I don't lose him before I get him on the rocks!" answered Jack. But his fears were groundless, for a few seconds later the catch lay at his feet—a fish weighing at least a pound and a half.

"That's the way to do it," said Randy.

"You might have had him—if you had cast in first," answered his companion, modestly.

"I'll try my luck now," and Randy cast in without delay. Then Jack also tried it again, and both boys began to fish in earnest. Soon Randy got a bite and brought in a fish weighing as much as the first catch.

"Now we are even," said Jack.

In an hour Randy had four good-sized fish to his credit and Jack had an equal number. Then Jack's luck fell away and Randy got three more while his companion got nothing.

"There is no use of talking, you are a better fisherman than I," said Jack.

"I think you drop down too deep," answered Randy. "Try it this way," and he showed his friend what he meant.

After that Jack's success was a trifle better, but still Randy kept ahead of him.

When the boys had caught twenty fish between them they decided to give up the sport. Randy knew where they could find some blackberries, and leaving their fish in a hole among the rocks, where there was a small pool of water, they tramped away from the river to where the blackberry bushes were located.

"These are fine," said Jack, eating a handful with a relish. "Randy, we ought to come berrying here some day."

"I am willing."

"These berries would make the nicest kind of pies."

"Yes, indeed! And if there is anything I love it is a good, juicy blackberry pie."

"If we had a kettle we might take some home with us now."

"I am afraid it is too late. What time is it?"

Jack carried a neat silver watch which he consulted.

"Why, it's half-past five already! I thought it might be four. Yes, we'll have to get back."

"Let us go down to the boat first and then row up and get the fish."

This suited the two boys, and soon they were

making their way back over the rocks to where Jack's craft had been left. As they came out from among the trees and bushes they saw another boat on the river, headed for Riverport.

"There is Bob Bangs again!" exclaimed Randy.

"Hullo!" yelled Jack. "Have you been fishing, too?"

"Yes," answered the big boy, and continued to row down the river.

"Have any luck?" went on Jack.

"Fine," was the short answer, and then Bob Bangs' craft drew out of hearing.

"He was in a tremendous hurry," mused Jack.

"Perhaps he didn't want us to see what he had caught," answered Randy.

"That's likely it, Randy. I don't believe he knows as much about fishing as I do—and that is little enough."

Having secured the rowboat, Randy and Jack rowed up to the fishing hole, and Randy scrambled up the rocks to secure their two strings of fish. He soon reached the shallow pool among the rocks in which they had been placed and drew up the two strings.

"Well, I declare!" he ejaculated, as he

looked the fish over. Then he counted them carefully. "What can this mean?"

His string had held twelve fish and Jack's eight fish. Now three of the largest fish from each string were gone. He looked around with care, but could see nothing of the missing fish.

"Hullo! What's keeping you?" shouted Jack, from the boat.

"Come up here!" called back Randy.

"Anything wrong?"

"Yes."

"Landy! I hope the fish aren't gone!" burst out Jack, as he scrambled up the rocks and ran to where Randy was continuing the search.

The situation was soon explained and both boys hunted around in the neighborhood of the pool, thinking the fish might have gotten away in some manner. Then of a sudden Jack uttered a cry:

"Look at this, Randy!"

"What is it?"

"A key ring, with two keys on it."

"Where did you find it?"

"Here, right beside the pool."

"Then somebody has been here and taken our fish!"

"Exactly what I believe."

Jack began to examine the key ring and then he uttered another exclamation:

"Here are some initials on the ring."

"What are they?"

"I can't make out very well—they are so worn. I think the first is R."

"Let me see."

Jack passed the find over and Randy examined it.

"I can make it out," said Randy. "R. A. B."

"Robert A. Bangs!" shouted Jack.

"Bob Bangs!" murmured Randy. "Could he have been mean enough to come here and take some of our fish?"

"It certainly looks that way."

"Let us go after him and find out."

"All right. Anyway, we can make him explain how his key ring got here."

Taking what was left of the fish, the two boys hurried back to the rowboat and soon each was seated at an oar and pulling a good stroke in the direction of the town.

"He must have been watching us fish," observed Jack. "And he must have seen us place our catch in the pool."

"And took our best fish because he couldn't catch any of his own," concluded Randy. "Well, if he has my fish he has got to give them up," he added, with determination.

Rowing at a good rate of speed, it did not take the boys long to reach the town. As they moved past one dock after another they looked for Bob Bangs, but the big youth was nowhere in sight.

"I reckon he was afraid of being followed," said Jack.

"There is his boat," answered Randy, and pointed to the craft, which was tied up near an old boathouse and not at the regular Bangs dock.

While the two boys rested on their oars an old man who was lame, and who rented out boats for a living, came from the old boathouse. "Hullo, Isaac!" called out Jack. "Have you seen Bob Bangs around here?"

"Why, yes; he just went ashore," answered Isaac Martin.

"Did he have any fish?"

"Yes, a nice string—some pretty big ones, too."

"How many?"

"Seven or eight."

"Which way did he go?"

"Up Samson Street."

"That's the back way to his house," cried Randy. "Come on!"

"What shall we do with our fish and the boat?"

"Let Isaac take care of them."

"Want me to take care of things, eh?" said the lame boatman. "Very well, I'll do it."

The two boys were soon on the way, on a run. They knew about the route Bob Bangs would take to get home and came in sight of the big boy just as he was entering his father's garden by a rear gate.

"Stop, Bob!" called out Randy.

The big boy looked around hastily and was much chagrined to see the others so close at hand. He held his string of fish behind him.

"What do you want?" he demanded, as they came closer.

"You know well enough what we want," returned Jack. "We want our fish."

"Your fish? Who has got your fish?" blustered Bob.

"You've got them," retorted Randy, and made a snatch at the string. The big boy held fast and a regular tug of war ensued.

"Let go!"

"I won't!"

"You shall!"

"See here, Bob," interposed Jack. "It won't

do you any good to hang on. Those are our fish and we want them."

"Bah! How do you know they are your fish?"

"Because you took them from the pool in which we placed them."

"I did not."

"You did."

"You can't prove it."

"Yes, we can."

"How?"

"By this," said Jack, triumphantly, and exhibited the key ring and keys.

CHAPTER III

EXPOSING BOB BANGS

When Bob Bangs saw the key ring his face changed color.

"Where did you get that?" he demanded.

"Got it where you dropped it—at the pool where we left our fish."

"How do you know it is mine?"

"By the initials on it."

"Humph!"

"If you don't want the key ring we'll keep it," put in Randy, quickly.

"No, you won't keep it. Give it to me."

"Then give us our fish," said Randy, quietly but firmly.

"They are not all your fish. I caught two of them."

"The two smallest, I suppose."

"No, the two largest."

"We lost six big fish and these belong to us," said Randy, and took the best fish from the string.

"Bob Bangs, it was a contemptible thing to do," he added, with spirit. "I wouldn't do such a dirty thing for a thousand dollars."

"Bah! Don't talk to me, unless you want to get hurt," growled the large youth, savagely.

"I am not afraid of you, even if you are bigger than I am," said Randy, undaunted by the fighting attitude the bully had assumed.

"It certainly was a mean piece of business," came from Jack. "If you wanted some fish why didn't you ask us for them?"

"Humph! I can buy my fish if I want to."

"Then why did you take ours?" demanded Randy.

"I—er—I didn't know they belonged to you. I just saw the strings in the pool and took a few," answered the boy, lamely. "Give me my key ring."

The ring with the keys was passed over, and Randy and Jack restrung their fish. In the meantime Bob Bangs entered his father's garden, slamming the gate after him.

"You just wait—I'll get square with you!" he shouted back, and shook his fist at Randy.

"You be careful, or you'll get into trouble!" shouted back Randy, and then he and Jack walked away with their fish.

"What's the matter, Master Robert?" asked the man-of-all-work around the Bangs place, as he approached Bob from the barn.

"Oh, some fellows are getting fresh," grumbled the big youth. "But I'll fix them for it!"

"I see they took some of your fish."

"We had a dispute about the fish. Rather than take them from such a poor chap as Randy Thompson I let him keep them," said Bob, glibly. "But I am going to get square with him for his impudence," he added.

After a long hard row and fishing for over an hour, Bob Bangs had caught only two small fish and he was thoroughly disgusted with everything and everybody. He walked into the kitchen and threw the fish on the sink board.

"There, Mamie, you can clean those and fry them for my supper," he said to the servant girl.

"Oh, land sakes, Master Bob, they are very small," cried the girl. "They won't go around nohow!"

"I said you could fry them for *my* supper," answered Bob, coldly.

"They are hardly worth bothering with," murmured the servant girl, but the boy did not hear her, for he had passed to the next room. He went upstairs and washed up and then walked into the sitting room, where his mother reclined on a sofa, reading the latest novel of society life.

"Where is father?" he asked, abruptly.

"I do not know, Robert," answered Mrs. Bangs, without looking up from her book.

"Will he be home to supper?"

To this there was no reply.

"I say, will he be home to supper?" and the boy shoved the book aside.

"Robert, don't be rude!" cried Mrs. Bangs, in irritation. "I presume he will be home," and she resumed her novel reading.

"I want some money."

To this there was no reply. Mrs. Bangs was on the last chapter of the novel and wanted to finish it before supper was served. She did little in life but read novels, dress, and attend parties, and she took but small interest in Bob and his doings.

"I say, I want some money," repeated the boy, in a louder key.

"Robert, will you be still? Every time I try to read you come and interrupt me."

"And you never want to listen to me. You read all the time."

"No, I do not—I really read very little, I have so many things to attend to. What did you say you wanted?"

"I want some money. I haven't had a cent this week."

"Then you must ask your father. I haven't anything to give you," and again Mrs. Bangs turned to her book.

"Can't you give me a dollar?"

Again there was no answer.

"I say, can't you give me a dollar?"

"I cannot. Now go away and be quiet until supper time."

"Then give me fifty cents."

"I haven't a penny. Ask your father."

"Oh, you're a mean thing!" growled the wayward son, and stalked out of the sitting room, slamming the door after him.

"What a boy!" sighed the lady of the house. "He never considers my comfort—and after all I have done for him!" And then she turned once more to her precious novel.

It wanted half an hour to supper time and Bob, not caring to do anything else, took himself back to his room. Like his mother, he, too, loved to read. Stowed away in a trunk, he had a score or more of cheap paper-covered novels, of daring adventures among the Indians, and of alluring detective tales, books on which he had squandered many a dime. One was called "Bowery Bob, the

Boy Detective of the Docks; or, Winning a Cool Million," and he wanted to finish this, to see how Bob got the million dollars. The absurdity of the stories was never noticed by him, and he thought them the finest tales ever penned.

He was deep in a chapter where the hero in rags was holding three men with pistols at bay when he heard a noise below and saw his father leaping from the family carriage. Mr. Bangs' face wore a look of great satisfaction, showing plainly that his day's business had agreed with him.

"How do you do, dad?" he said, running down to greet his parent.

"First-rate, Bob," said Mr. Bangs, with a smile. "How have things gone with you to-day?"

"Not very well."

"What's the matter?"

"You forgot to give me my spending money this week."

"I thought I gave it to you Saturday."

"That was for last week."

"I think you are mistaken, Bob. However, it doesn't matter much," went on Mr. Bangs, as he entered the house.

"Phew! He's in a fine humor to-night,"

thought Bob. "I'll have to strike him for more than a dollar."

"Where's your mother?" went on the gentleman.

"In the sitting room, reading. But I say, dad, what about that money?"

"Oh, do you want it right away?"

"I'd like to have it after supper."

"Very well."

"Can I have three dollars? I want to buy something extra this week—some things I really need."

"Ahem! Three dollars is quite a sum. I don't know of any other boy in Riverport who gets as much as three dollars in one week to spend."

"Well, but they haven't as rich a father as I have."

"Ah, quite true," nodded Mr. Bangs, with satisfaction. "I think I can safely lay claim to being the richest man in this district."

"Then I can have the three dollars?" went on Bob, anxiously.

"Yes. Here you are," and his parent brought forth a well-filled wallet and handed over three new one-dollar bills.

Bob was stowing the money away in his pocket

and congratulating himself on his luck when a door opened and Mrs. Bangs appeared.

"So you are back, Amos," she said, sweetly. "It has been such a long, lonesome day without you."

"And a busy day for me," answered Amos Bangs, as he passed into the sitting room and dropped into an easy chair.

"Did you go to Springfield?"

"I did, and met Tuller and the rest. We've got that thing in our grip now."

"Yes," she said, vaguely. In reality she took no interest whatever in her husband's affairs so long as she got what money she desired.

"Yes, sir—we've got the thing just where we want it," continued Amos Bangs.

"You mean——?" his wife hesitated.

"I mean that iron works affair of course, Viola. Can't you understand at all?"

"Oh—er—yes, of course. Let me see, you were trying to get control so you said."

"Exactly, and I've got it."

"Was not that the works in which Mr. Bartlett is interested?"

"The same."

"Did not he have the control?"

"Yes, but I have it now, and I am going to

keep it," answered Amos Bangs, with evident satisfaction.

"Do you mean Jack Bartlett's father, dad?" questioned Bob, eagerly.

"I do."

"Have you got the best of him."

"Well, I have—ahem—carried my point and the iron works will be absorbed by the concern in Springfield."

"And Jack Bartlett's father won't like that?"

"No. In fact, I am afraid he will fight it. But he can do nothing, absolutely nothing," went on Amos Bangs. "I hold the whip hand—and I shall continue to hold it."

"I hate the Bartletts and I hope you do get the best of them."

"This will make Mrs. Bartlett take a back seat," said Mrs. Bangs, maliciously.

"Maybe you mean that seat in church," said Bob, slyly.

"Not that particularly, although it is time they went to the rear—they have had a front seat so long. Amos, we must take a front seat now."

"As you please, Viola."

"And I must have some new dresses."

"You shall have them, my dear."

"You dear, good man!" cried the fashionable

wife; and then the whole family went in to supper. Bob felt particularly elated. He had gotten three dollars for spending money and he felt sure that the Bartletts, including Jack, would have to suffer.

"I wish dad could do something to injure the Thompsons," he said to himself. "But Mr. Thompson is only a carpenter. I must watch my chance and get square with Randy on my own account."

CHAPTER IV

RANDY AT HOME

ALL unmindful of the trouble that had already come to the Bartletts, and of the trouble Bob Bangs was hatching out for him, Randy divided the mess of fish with Jack and hurried home.

"See what a fine mess I've got, mother!" he cried, as he entered the kitchen, where his mother had just started to prepare the evening meal. "Aren't they real beauties?"

"They are, Randy," answered Mrs. Thompson, and smiled brightly. "Did Jack do as well?"

"Almost as well as I did, and we divided evenly, because, you see, he furnished the boat. And, mother, I've found out where we can get a fine lot of blackberries. If you want me to, I'll go for them to-morrow."

"I wish you would, Randy. Your father loves blackberry pie and blackberry pudding."

"And so do I."

"I've got time to fry some of these fish for supper," went on Mrs. Thompson. "And we can have some more to-morrow, too. But I don't think we can use them all."

"I was thinking we might give Mrs. Gilligan a couple."

"That will be very nice. If you will, take them over at once."

Mrs. Gilligan was a poor Irishwoman who took in washing and ironing for a living. She was alone in the world and often had a struggle to make both ends meet.

"Just to look at that now!" she cried, as Randy held up the fish. "Sure an' ye air a great fisher b'y, Randy, so ye air!"

"I got so many I thought I'd bring you a couple," said our hero.

"Now that's rale kind of ye," answered Mrs. Gilligan, as she dried her hands and took the fish. "Just loike my Pat used to catch afore he was kilt on the railroad."

"I caught them this afternoon, so you can be sure they are fresh."

"I'm much obliged to ye, I am indade," said Mrs. Gilligan. She drew a long breath. "Sure an' the Lord is good to us after all. I was just afther thinkin' I had nothin' but throuble, whin in comes these iligant fish."

"Is something wrong?" asked Randy, curiously.

"It's not a great dale, yet it's enough fer a poor woman loike me. It's Mrs. Bangs' wash, so it is. Nothin' suits that lady, an' she always wants to pay less than she agreed."

"You mean Bob Bangs' mother?"

"Th' same, Randy. Oh, they are a hard-hearted family, so they are!"

"I believe you. And yet Mr. Bangs is rich."

"It's little enough I see of his money," sighed Mrs. Gilligan. "Although I do me besht wid the washin' an' ironin', so I do!"

"It's a wonder Mrs. Bangs don't make the servant do the washing and ironing."

"She did make the other wan do that same. But the new one can't iron an' won't try, so I have the work, an' the girrul gits less wages," answered the Irishwoman.

When Randy returned home he found supper almost ready. The appetizing odor of frying fish filled the air. A few minutes later Mr. Thompson came in.

Louis Thompson was a man a little past middle age, tall and thin and not unlike Randy in the general appearance of his face. He was not a strong man, and the winter before had been laid up with a severe attack of rheumatism.

"That smells good," he said, with a smile, as he kissed his wife. "I like fish."

"Randy just caught them."

"Good enough."

"You look tired, Louis," went on Mrs. Thompson. "Was the work extra hard?"

"Not much harder than usual, Lucy, but I was working on a cellar partition and it was very damp. It brought back a bit of the rheumatism."

"That is too bad."

"Can't the boss give you something else to do —something where it isn't damp?" questioned Randy.

"I have asked him about it," answered his father. "But just at present there is nothing else in sight."

"You must take care, Louis," said Mrs. Thompson. "It will not do to risk having the rheumatism come back."

"I wish I could get something to do," said Randy, while the evening meal was in progress. "I might earn some money and it would help. But there doesn't seem to be any kind of an opening in Riverport."

"Times are rather dull," answered Mr. Thompson. "And I am afraid they will be worse before they are better."

On the following day Randy went out after blackberries. Jack went with him and the boys went up the stream in the latter's boat.

"If I can get a good mess mother is going to preserve some," said Randy.

"I like blackberry jam," answered his friend.

The two boys had brought their lunch with them, intending to remain out all day. By noon they had picked twelve quarts of berries and then sat down by the river side to eat their lunch.

"What do you say to a swim?" remarked Jack, after the meal was over.

"Just the thing!" cried our hero. "But we mustn't remain in longer than half an hour. I want to pick more berries."

They were soon in the water, which was deliciously cool and refreshing. They dove and splashed around to their hearts' content and raced from one bank to the other and back. Randy won the race by several seconds.

"I declare, Randy, you are a regular water rat!" declared Jack. "I never saw a better swimmer."

"Well, I do love the water, that is certain," answered Randy.

"And you row such a good stroke, too."

"That's because I love boats."

The half-hour at an end, our hero leaped ashore and began to don his garments, and Jack did the same. They were just finishing their toilet when a rowboat came into view, containing Bob Bangs and several other of the loud boys of Riverport.

"There is Bob Bangs again," whispered Randy.

"We'll have to watch out that he doesn't try to rob us of our berries," whispered Jack, significantly.

"Humph! Up here again, eh?" remarked the big youth, resting on his oars.

"We are," answered Randy. "I think we can come, if we please."

"Certainly—for all I care," growled Bob.

"We are picking berries, and we intend to watch them, too," put in Randy, loudly.

At this pointed remark Bob Bangs colored slightly.

"I should think you'd pick your company, Jack Bartlett," he said, coarsely.

"I do. That is why I am not with you."

"Humph!"

"I consider myself just as good as you, Bob Bangs," said Randy, warmly. "I may not be as rich, but I never tried to steal a mess of fish from anybody."

"You shut up!" roared the big boy. And then he started to row away.

"You'll not get a chance to rob us of these berries," called out Jack after him.

"What do they mean about robbing somebody of fish?" asked one of Bob's companions.

"Oh, that was only a joke," answered the rich youth. "Just wait—I'll fix them for it!"

As soon as Bangs and his cronies had disappeared Randy and Jack went back to their berry picking. They worked steadily until five o'clock in the afternoon, and by that time had a great number of quarts to their credit.

"The folks at home will be pleased," said Jack. "My mother loves fresh berries. She says they are much better than those which are several days in the market."

"And she is right."

The boys had brought along several large and small kettles, and had left three of these down near the boat, filled with the fruit. Each walked to the shore with a kettle full of berries in his hand.

"Well, I never!" cried Jack, in dismay.

"Bob Bangs again!" murmured Randy. "Oh,

don't I just wish I had him here. I'd pummel him good!"

There was good cause for our hero's anger. On the rocks lay the overturned berry kettles, the berries scattered in all directions and many of them crushed under foot.

"And look at the boat!" gasped Jack, turning to inspect the craft.

The rowboat was partly filled with water and on the seats and in the bottom a quantity of mud had been thrown. The oars were sticking in a mud bank close by.

"Does she leak?" asked our hero, with concern.

"I'll have to find out."

It was soon discovered that the craft was intact, and then they set to work to clean up the muss. This was no easy job, and the boys perspired freely, for the day was a warm one. Then Randy looked over the scattered berries.

"About one-third of them are fit to take along," he said. "The others are crushed and dirty."

"I'll tell you what I am going to do," said Jack, stoutly. "I am going to make Bob Bangs pay for dirtying my boat, and he can pay for the lost berries, too."

"But how can we prove he is guilty?"

"We'll make him own up to it. Nobody else would play such a mean trick."

The two boys were in no happy frame of mind as they rowed back to Riverport. They suspected that Bob Bangs would keep out of their sight, but just as they were landing they caught sight of him peering at them from behind a dock building.

"There he is!" cried Jack. "After him, Randy!"

"Right you are!" answered our hero, and ran after Bob Bangs with might and main. Randy was a good sprinter and although the rich youth tried to get away he was soon brought to a halt.

"Let go of me!" he roared, as Randy caught him by the collar.

"Not just yet, Bob Bangs!" returned Randy. "A fine trick you played this afternoon."

"I didn't play any trick!"

"Yes, you did."

"I didn't! Let me go!" And now Bob Bangs did his best to get away. He saw that Randy and Jack were thoroughly angry and was afraid he was in for a drubbing—or worse. He gave a jerk and then started to run. Randy put out his foot and the big youth went sprawling full length, his face violently striking the ground.

CHAPTER V

THE RESULT OF A QUARREL

If any boy was ever humiliated it was Bob Bangs. His face and hands were covered with dust and so was his elegant suit of clothing, while the skin was cut on the side of his nose.

"Now, see what you have done!" he spluttered, gazing ruefully at himself. "My suit is just about ruined!"

"And it serves you right, Bob Bangs," came warmly from Jack.

"That is what you get for trying to run away," added our hero.

"I'll have the law on you, Randy Thompson!"

"Maybe I'll have the law on you, Bob Bangs!"

"You had no right to throw me down in that fashion."

"Then why did you start to run away?"

"Because I didn't want to stay here—and you had no right to stop me."

"We wanted to know about this berry affair," said Jack. "And about the dirty boat."

"I don't know what you are talking about," answered the big boy, but his face showed his concern.

"You put mud in my boat and spilled our berries."

"Who says I did that?"

"We know you did."

"Did you see us?"

"No, but we know you did it and nobody else."

"You can't prove it," answered Bob, and now his face showed a sign of relief. He had been afraid that there had been a witness of his evil-doing.

"Perhaps we can," said Randy. "Bob Bangs, I think you are the meanest boy in Riverport!" he continued, with spirit.

"I don't care what you think, Randy Thompson. Who are you, anyway? The son of a poor carpenter. Why, you haven't got a decent suit of clothing to your back!"

"For shame, Bob!" broke in Jack. "Randy is a good fellow, even if he is poor."

"Well, if you think he is so good you can go with him. But I don't want to associate with such a low fellow," went on the big youth, as he started to brush himself off with a silk handkerchief.

"So I am a low fellow, am I?" said Randy, in a steady voice, and coming up close to Bob, who promptly began to back away.

"Ye—as, you—you are," stammered the rich youth.

"I've a good mind to knock you down for saying it, Bob Bangs. I am not as low as you."

"Humph!"

"I would never do the low things you have done. It was a mean, contemptible trick that you played on Jack and me. By right you ought to be made to scrub out the boat and pay for the berries you spoiled."

"Bah! I won't touch the boat, and I won't pay a cent."

"Then you admit that you are guilty?"

"I admit that I had some fun, at your expense, yes," answered Bob Bangs. "You can't do anything to me, though, for you can't prove it against me."

"That means, if you were brought up into court, you would lie about it," said Randy.

"Humph! You needn't get so personal, Randy Thompson."

"For two pins, do you know what I would do, Bob Bangs?"

"What?"

"I'd give you a good thrashing," and Randy pulled up his sleeves, as if he meant to begin operations at once.

"No! no! Don't you—you dare to touch me!" gasped the rich boy, in alarm. "If you do, I'll—I'll have the law on you!"

"And we'll have the law on you."

Bob Bangs was more alarmed than ever. He saw that Randy was ready to pitch into him on the instant. He looked around, saw an opening, and darted away at his best speed.

"Let him go—the big coward," called out Jack, for Randy had started after the rich boy. "We can settle with him another time."

"What a mean chap!" cried Randy. "I never saw his equal, never!"

Bob Bangs ran a distance of several rods. Then, seeing a clod of dirt lying in the road, he picked it up and hurled it at the boys. He was not a good thrower, but as luck would have it the clod struck Randy on the shoulder, some of the dirt spattering up into his ear.

"Ha! ha! That's the time you got it!" sang out the rich boy, gleefully.

RANDY CAUGHT BOB BANGS BY THE ARM, AND THREW HIM OVER ON HIS SIDE.—P. 49.

"And this is the time you are going to get it," returned Randy, and made a dash after him. Seeing this, Jack followed after the pair.

Bob Bangs could run and fear lent speed to his flying feet. But he was no match for Randy, who had on more than one occasion won a running match amongst his schoolfellows. Bob started for home, several blocks away, but just before he reached his gate Randy came near to him, caught him by the arm and flung him over on his side. Then, to hold him down, our hero seated himself on top of the rich boy, who began to bellow lustily.

"Get off of me!"

"I will not!"

"You are squeezing the wind out of me!"

"What right had you to throw that chunk of dirt at me?"

"I—er—I was only fooling."

"Maybe I am only fooling, too."

"You are breaking my ribs! Oh, let up, I say!"

"Are you sorry for what you did?" demanded Randy.

To this Bob Bangs made no reply.

"I see you've got him," said Jack, running up at that instant.

"Yes, and I am going to give it to him good," answered Randy.

"Let up! Help, somebody! Help!" roared Bob, badly frightened. He began to kick and struggle, but Randy held him down and as a consequence he was covered with dust and dirt from head to foot.

In the midst of the mêlée a carriage came along the roadway. It contained Mrs. Bangs and the man-of-all-work, who was driving.

"Mercy on us! What does this mean?" burst from the fashionable lady's lips. "Can that be Robert?"

"Help! help!" roared the rich youth, more lustily than ever.

"It certainly is Robert," went on Mrs. Bangs. "John, stop the carriage. You rude boy, let my son alone!" she went on, in her shrill, hard voice.

"Hullo, here is Mrs. Bangs," remarked Jack, looking around and discovering the new arrival.

For the instant Randy did not see the rich woman and continued to hold down Bob, who struggled violently, sending up a cloud of dust in the road. Then he noticed the carriage and looked up, and his face fell.

"You scamp! Leave my boy alone!" screamed Mrs. Bangs. "Oh, John, perhaps you had better run for a policeman!" she added, as Randy let go his hold and arose.

"You had better not, Mrs. Bangs," said Jack. "Bob deserves what he is getting."

"I do not believe it! It is disgraceful to throw him down in the road like this," stormed the fashionable lady.

"He hit Randy with a chunk of dirt."

"I—I didn't do nothing!" howled Bob, as he got up. He was too ruffled to think of his bad grammar.

"And that elegant suit is about ruined," went on Mrs. Bangs. "I never heard of such doings before. Boy," she went on, looking at Randy, "you ought to be locked up!"

"It is Bob ought to be locked up," retorted Randy. "He started this trouble; I didn't."

"I do not believe it. My son is a gentleman."

"I didn't do a thing," put in the rich boy, feeling safe, now that his mother and the hired man were on the scene. "They pitched into me for nothing at all."

"Bob knows better than that," said Jack.

"Yesterday he tried to steal some fish we caught, and to-day he mussed up Jack's boat and ruined some berries that both of us had picked," explained Randy. "I took him to task about it and then he threw the mud at me. Then I chased him and caught him, as you saw."

"Preposterous! My boy would not steal!" said Mrs. Bangs, tartly. She looked meaningly at Jack. "I presume you and your family are very bitter against us now," she added, significantly.

"Bitter against you?" said Jack, puzzled.

"Yes—because of that iron works affair."

"I don't know anything about that, Mrs. Bangs."

"Oh, then you haven't heard yet." The fashionable woman was nonplussed. "Never mind. You must leave Robert alone."

"Ain't you going to get that policeman and lock them up?" asked the son, anxiously.

"If I am locked up, you'll be locked up, too," said Randy. "And the charge against you will be stealing as well as malicious mischief."

"Yes, and we'll prove our case," added Jack. "Bob doesn't know what witnesses we have."

At this announcement Bob Bangs' face grew pale.

"Yo—you can't prove anything," he faltered.

"You don't know about that," said Randy, taking his cue from Jack.

"I will look into this affair later—just now I have no time," said Mrs. Bangs, after an awkward pause. "Robert, you had better go into the house and clean yourself up. John, you can drive on." And then, while the fashionable woman was driven into her grounds, her son lost no time in sneaking off into the house. As he entered the door he turned and shook his fist at our hero and Jack.

"Jack, I don't think we have heard the last of this," remarked Randy, as he and his companion started away.

"Perhaps not, but I think we have the best of it," answered Jack.

"I don't know about that. Mrs. Bangs is a very high-strung woman and thinks a good deal of Bob."

"I'd like to know what she meant about the iron works matter," went on Jack, with a troubled look on his face. "I hope Mr. Bangs hasn't got the best of father in that deal."

"You had better ask your father when you get home."

"I will."

The two lads hurried back to the boat and placed the craft where it belonged. Then the berries were divided, and each started for his home little dreaming of the trouble that was in store for both of them.

CHAPTER VI

THE IRON WORKS AFFAIR

When Jack arrived at home he took the berries around to the kitchen and then hurried upstairs to the bathroom, to wash and fix up for supper. He was in the midst of his ablutions when he heard his father come in and go to the library. An animated talk between his two parents followed.

"Something unusual is up," thought Jack, and went below as soon as he was fixed up.

He found his father sitting near the library table, his head resting on his hand. His face looked careworn. Mrs. Bartlett sat by an open window clasping her hands tightly. Their earnest talk came to a sudden end as Jack entered.

"Good-evening, father and mother," said the boy and then halted. "Maybe I was interrupting you," he added.

"Jack may as well know," said Mrs. Bartlett, looking meaningly at her husband.

"I suppose so," answered Mr. Bartlett, and gave a long sigh.

"Know what?" asked Jack.

"Your father has had trouble at the iron works," answered his mother.

"What kind of trouble?"

"It is the Bangs affair," answered Mr. Bartlett. "You know a little about that already. Well, Amos Bangs has forced me into a corner."

"What do you mean by that, father?"

"He has gained control of the company and is going to consolidate with the Springfield concern."

"Will that harm you much?"

"A great deal, I am afraid, Jack. In the past I have known all that was going on. Now I will have to rely on Amos Bangs—and I do not care to do that."

"Don't you think he is honest?"

"Privately, I do not, although I should not care to say so in public. He and his friends at Springfield are sharpers. They will squeeze what they can out of the new concern, and I am afraid I shall be left out in the cold."

"Well, I shouldn't trust Mr. Bangs myself. He and his son are of a stripe, and I know only too well now what Bob is."

"Have you had trouble with Bob?" questioned Mrs. Bartlett, quickly.

"Yes," answered Jack, and gave the particulars. "How Bob will crow over me now!" he went on, ruefully.

"This will make Bangs harder on me than ever," remarked Mr. Bartlett.

"Oh, I trust not, father!" cried Jack. "I am sure you have trouble enough already!"

"The Bangses are a hard family to get along with," said Mrs. Bartlett. "I have heard that from several who work for them."

"The men at the office are sorry to see Amos Bangs in control," said Mr. Bartlett. "They know he will drive them more than I have ever driven them, and he will never raise their wages."

"Are you going to leave the company's office, father?"

"Yes. I am no longer an officer, only a stockholder."

"The company ought to give you a position."

"Bangs said I could be a timekeeper, at fifteen dollars per week."

"How mean! And what will his salary be?"

"I don't know yet—probably a hundred and fifty per week—seven or eight thousand per year."

"And you've been getting sixty dollars per week, haven't you?"

"Yes."

"Then I'd go elsewhere."

"That is what I shall do—if I can find any opening. What I am worried about mostly is the capital I have in the iron works, fifteen thousand dollars. I am afraid Bangs will, sooner or later, wipe me out, and do it in such a way that I cannot sue him to advantage."

"It's an outrage!"

"The trouble is, I trusted him too much from the start. He has proved to be a snake in the grass."

"And Bob is exactly like him," said Jack.

The family talked the matter over all during the supper hour and for some time later. The prospect ahead was a dark one and Mrs. Bartlett sighed deeply.

"If you cannot get an opening elsewhere I do not know what we are to do," said she to her husband.

"I'll get something," he replied, bravely. "And remember, I have a thousand dollars in cash in the bank."

"A thousand dollars won't last long, Philip, after once you begin to use it up."

"That is true."

"Have you anything definite in view?"

"Not exactly. I am going to write to my friend Mason, in Albany. He may be able to get me something to do at the iron works there. He is in charge."

"Well, I hope it is better than the place Amos Bangs offered you."

"There is only one trouble," went on Mr. Bartlett. "If I get work at Albany we will have to move to that city."

"Well, we can do that."

"Yes, but I hate to go away from Riverport. I wanted to watch Bangs."

"You might go to Albany every Monday and come home Saturday night, at least for a time."

"Yes, I might do that," answered Philip Bartlett.

On the following morning he went down to the iron works as usual. As early as it was he found Amos Bangs ahead of him, and sorting out some papers at one of the desks.

"Morning," said Amos Bangs, curtly.

"Good-morning," answered Mr. Bartlett. "Mr. Bangs, what are you doing at this desk?"

"Sorting out things."

"Do you not know that this is my private desk?"

"Is it? I thought it belonged to the iron company," answered Amos Bangs with a sneer.

"The desk does belong to the company, but at present it contains my private papers as well as some papers of the company."

"Well, it is going to be my desk after this. I'll thank you to take your personal things away."

"You seem to be in a hurry to get me out."

"I want to get to work here. Things have dragged long enough. I am going to make them hum."

"I am glad to hear it," answered Philip Bartlett, pointedly. "I presume we can look for big dividends on our stock next year."

"Well—er—I don't know about that. We have got to make improvements and they will cost money."

"You didn't want any improvements when I was in charge."

"That was a different thing. The old concern was a small-fry affair. We are going to make the new concern something worth while," answered Amos Bangs, loftily.

"I hope you do—for my sake as well as for the

sake of the other stockholders. But what salaries are the new officers to have?"

"That is to be decided later."

"I trust all the profits are not eaten up by the salaries."

"You cannot expect talented men—like myself, for instance—to work for low salaries."

"You used to be willing to work for fifty dollars a week."

"Those days are past. But I cannot waste time talking now. Clean out the desk and turn it over to me," concluded Amos Bangs, and walked away.

With a heavy heart Philip Bartlett set about the task before him. He was much attached to the iron works and hated to leave it. Presently his brow grew troubled.

"Mr. Bangs!" he called.

"What do you want now?"

"Did you see anything of some papers with a broad rubber band around them?"

"Didn't see anything but what is there."

"I had some private papers. They seem to be gone."

"I didn't take them," answered Amos Bangs, coldly.

"It is queer where they can be," went on Philip Bartlett.

"Well, I haven't got them."

Philip Bartlett hunted high and low for the missing documents, but without success. Then he cleaned out the desk, put his personal things in a package, said good-by to his former employees, and quit the office.

"I am well rid of him," said Amos Bangs, to himself. "And I am glad I got hold of those private contracts. Now I can make a deal with Shaster and turn the work over to the Springfield concern—and make some money!"

CHAPTER VII

MORE TROUBLES FOR RANDY

Two days passed quietly, and Randy did not see or hear anything more of Bob Bangs. Then he learned through Jack that Mrs. Bangs had gone off on a summer trip, taking her son with her.

"I hear there are great changes at the iron works," said Randy, to his friend. "Mr. Bangs, they say, is in charge."

"He is, and father is out of it," answered Jack, bitterly. "That is what Mrs. Bangs meant when she said I must be bitter against the family."

"Is your father out of it entirely, Jack?"

"Yes, so far as holding a position is concerned. He still has his stock. But he is afraid that won't be worth much, if Amos Bangs runs the concern."

"What is your father going to do?"

"He doesn't know yet. He is trying to connect with some other iron works."

"I hope he strikes something good."

"So do I, Randy."

"I wish I could get something to do, too," went on Randy.

"You mean during the summer?"

"Yes, and maybe later, too."

"Why, isn't your father working?"

"Not to-day. He has been working in a damp cellar and that brought on his old complaint, rheumatism. He suffers something awful with it. He ought to have a long rest."

"He certainly ought not to work in a cellar."

"He has already told his boss he couldn't go at it again," answered Randy.

"Have you had a doctor?"

"Yes, Doctor Case came this morning."

"What does he say?"

"He says rheumatism is hard to cure and that my father will have to take care of himself," answered Randy. "But I must go on now," he added. "I must get some things for mother at the store."

What Randy said about his father was true. Louis Thompson was suffering very much. He rested on a couch in the sitting room of the cottage, and his wife did what she could to relieve his pain.

Several days passed and the rheumatism, instead of growing better, became worse, so that neither Mrs. Thompson nor Randy knew what to do for the sufferer. Then Mr. Thompson's side began to draw up, and in haste a specialist from the city was called in. He gave some relief, but said it would be a long time before the sufferer would be able to go to work again.

"You must keep off your left leg," said the specialist.

A few days after that Louis Thompson tried to walk. But the pain was so great he could not stand on the rheumatic limb. He sank on his couch with a groan.

"I cannot do it," he gasped.

"Then do not try," answered his wife.

"But I must get to work, Lucy. I cannot afford to be idle."

"Never mind, Louis; we will get along somehow."

"How much did that specialist charge?"

"Fifty dollars?"

"And what was Doctor Case's bill?"

"Ten dollars."

"Sixty dollars! And we had only ninety dollars in the bank! That leaves us only thirty dollars."

To this Mrs. Thompson did not answer. She

had used up nearly ten dollars for medicines, but did not wish to worry her suffering husband by mentioning it.

"If I don't go to work we'll all starve to death!" continued Louis Thompson.

"We'll manage somehow," answered the wife, bravely.

Nevertheless, she was much discouraged, and that evening, when her husband was asleep, she and Randy talked the matter over as they sat on the porch in the darkness.

"Mother," said Randy, earnestly, "I don't want you to feel troubled. You have labored so long for me that it is now my turn. I only want something to do."

"My dear child," said the mother, "I do not need to be assured of your willingness. But I am sorry that you should be compelled to give up your vacation and maybe your schooling."

"Giving up schooling will not be necessary. I can study in the evenings. I am wondering what I can find to do."

"I know so little about such things, Randy, that we must consult someone who is better qualified to give advice in the matter—your Uncle Peter, for instance."

At this Randy gave a sigh.

"I don't know Uncle Peter. He never comes here."

"That is true," answered Mrs. Thompson, with some hesitation. "But you know he is a business man and has a great deal to attend to. Besides, he has married a lady who is exceedingly fashionable, and I suppose he does not care to bring her to visit such unfashionable folks as we are."

"Then," said Randy, indignantly, "I don't want to trouble him with any of my applications. If he doesn't think us good enough to visit we won't force ourselves upon him."

"My dear boy, you are too excitable. It may be that it is only his business engagements that have kept him away from us. Besides, you can go to him only for advice; it is quite different from asking assistance."

Mother and son discussed the situation for fully an hour and at last, in the absence of other plans, it was decided that Randy should go to his uncle the next day and make known his wants. Mr. Thompson was told, early in the morning, and said Randy could do as he thought best.

"But don't expect too much from your Uncle Peter," said the sick man.

Peter Thompson was an elder brother to

Randy's father. Early in life he had entered a counting room and ever since had been engaged in mercantile pursuits. At the age of twenty-eight he had married a dashing lady, who was more noted for her fashionable pretensions than for any attractive qualities of the heart. She was now at the head of a very showy establishment, far more pretentious than that over which Mrs. Bangs presided. She knew little about her husband's relations and cared still less.

The town of Riverport was twenty miles distant from Deep Haven, where Peter Thompson resided with his family. A boat ran daily between these places and several others, but Randy did not wish to spend the necessary fare, and so borrowed a bicycle from Jack and made the trip by way of the river road, a safe if not very comfortable highway.

Randy had been to Deep Haven several times in years gone by, but, strange as it may seem, had never gone near his uncle's residence. But he knew where the house was located—a fine brick affair, with a swell front—and leaning his bicycle against a tree, he mounted the stone steps and rang the bell.

"What's wanted?" demanded the servant who answered the summons, and she looked Randy over in a supercilious manner, not at all impressed by the modest manner in which he was attired.

"Is Uncle Peter at home?" asked Randy, politely.

"Who's Uncle Peter?"

"Mr. Peter Thompson?"

"No, he isn't."

"Where is he?"

"At his store, I expect."

"Is Mrs. Thompson at home?"

"I don't know. I'll see. Who shall I say wants to see her?"

"Randy Thompson."

Randy was left standing in the elegantly furnished hallway while the servant departed. He could not help but contrast such elegance with his own modest home.

"Come into the drawing room," said the servant, briefly, on returning, and ushered him into the finest apartment he had ever entered.

Here he was kept waiting for fully quarter of an hour. Then a showily dressed woman swept into the room with a majestic air and fixed a cold stare upon our hero.

"Are you my aunt?" he asked, somewhat disconcerted by his chilling reception.

"Really, I couldn't say—not having seen you before," she answered.

"My name is Randy Thompson. I am the son of Louis Thompson, of Riverport."

"Ah, I see."

The woman said no more, but seemed to await developments. Randy was greatiy embarrassed. His aunt's coldness repelled him, and he easily saw that he was not a welcome visitor. A touch of pride came to him and he resolved that he would be as unsociable as his relative.

"What can he want of me?" thought the woman.

As Randy said nothing more she grew tired of the stillness and drew herself up once more.

"You must excuse me this morning," she said. "I am particularly engaged. I suppose you know where your uncle's store is. You will probably find him there." And then she rang for the servant to show our hero to the door. He was glad to get out into the open air once more.

"So that is Aunt Grace," he mused. "Well, I don't know as I shall ever wish to call upon her again. She is as bad as an iceberg for freezing a fellow. No wonder she and mother have never become friends."

CHAPTER VIII

RANDY AND HIS UNCLE PETER

FROM his uncle's home Randy rode on his bicycle to Peter Thompson's store—a fairly large concern, the largest, in fact, in Deep Haven. He found his uncle behind a desk in the rear, busy over some accounts. For several minutes he paid no attention to his visitor. Then he stuck his pen behind his ear and gave Randy a sharp look.

"How do you do, Uncle Peter?" said the youth.

"Why—er—who is this?" stammered Peter Thompson. "I don't seem to quite know you."

"I am Randy Thompson, your nephew."

"Oh, yes, my younger brother Louis' son, I believe."

"Yes, sir."

"I remember you now." Peter Thompson held out a flabby and cold hand. "Come to town on business, I suppose."

"In a way, yes, sir. Father is down with rheumatism."

"Hum! Didn't take proper care of himself, I suppose."

"He had to work in a cellar and that put him in bed."

"And you have come to ask help, I suppose." Peter Thompson's face dropped quickly. "I am sorry, but my family expenses are very large, and trade is dull. If I were able——"

"You are mistaken," said Randy, a flush mounting to his brow. "I do not come for assistance. I am old enough to work, if I only knew what to do. Mother told me to come to you for advice."

Peter Thompson looked relieved when he understood that Randy's visit meant no demand upon his purse, and he regarded the youth more favorably than he had done.

"Ah, that's well," he said, rubbing his flabby hands together. "I like your independence. *Now,* let me see." He scratched his head. "Do you know anything about horses?"

"No, sir; but perhaps I could learn."

"The livery-stable keeper wants a boy, but he must know all about horses."

"How much would he pay a week?"

"Two dollars at the start."

"That would not be enough for me."

"I might get you in some store in the city," continued Peter Thompson. "Would you like that?"

"If it paid, yes."

"It would pay but little the first year. But you would gain a valuable experience."

"I cannot afford that, Uncle Peter. I must earn something at once, to support our family."

"Then I don't know what can be done," said the storekeeper, with a shrug of his shoulders. "There are very few things that boys of your age can do, and it is so easy to obtain boys that people are not willing to pay much in wages."

Randy looked crestfallen and his uncle embarrassed. The merchant feared that he might be compelled by the world's opinion to aid his brother and his family. But suddenly an idea struck him.

"Do you know anything about farming?" he inquired.

"Yes, sir," said Randy; "a little."

"I ask for this reason," pursued Mr. Thompson. "When your grandfather died he left to me a small farm in Riverport. It is not very good and has been used mostly as a pasture. I have been so occupied with other things that I could not look after it. Perhaps you may know something of it."

"Yes, sir, I do. It is about half a mile from our house, and is called the twelve-acre lot. But I didn't know it belonged to you."

"It does. What I was going to say is that, although I am unable to give you such assistance as I should like, I will, if you wish it, give you the use of that lot, and the little cottage on it, rent-free so long as you care to use it. Perhaps you can put it to some use. Anyway, you can use the cottage."

Randy's face lighted up, much to his uncle's satisfaction. The land was not extra good and the cottage all but tumbled down, yet it was better than nothing. They could move out of the cottage in which they were now located, and thus save the monthly rent, which was eight dollars. Besides that, Randy felt that he could do something with the garden, even though it was rather late in the season. Where they now lived there was little room to grow vegetables.

"You are sure you don't want to use the place, Uncle Peter?" he asked.

"Not at all. You can use it as long as you please."

"Maybe you would like to sell it."

"Ahem! If you wish to buy it you can make an offer after you are on the place. I once offered it to a man for two hundred dollars, but he would not take me up."

"Then you will sell it for two hundred dollars?"

"I will sell it to you, or rather your father, for a hundred and fifty dollars."

"I'll remember that, sir. It may be that we will like the place so much we shall want to buy—if we can raise the money."

"You can pay off the amount at the rate of fifty dollars per year if you wish."

"Thank you. You are kind and I appreciate it," and Randy meant what he said.

Peter Thompson looked at the clock.

"I must go to dinner now. Will you dine with me?"

Had his uncle been alone Randy might have accepted the offer, but he remembered the reception his aunt had given him and so declined.

"I think I had better get back to Riverport," he said. "I will tell mother and father about the twelve-acre lot and see what they have to say about it."

"Very well."

"Would you mind giving me a slip of paper so

that we can prove we have a right to occupy the place?" pursued Randy. "Some folks may try to dispute our right. I know one man who pastures cows there."

"He has no right to do so. Here, I will give you a paper in due form."

Whatever his other shortcomings, Peter Thompson was not a slipshod business man. He drew up a paper in due form, stating that his brother could occupy the little farm for five years, rent-free, and if he wished to do so could at any time in said five years buy the little farm for one hundred and fifty dollars, payable at the rate of fifty dollars per year, without interest.

"And now good-by and good luck to you," said he as he handed the paper to Randy. "Some day, if I can get the time, I may call upon you. But I rarely go away from home."

Randy shook hands and left, and in a minute more was riding home on the bicycle.

"Well, I think I've gained something," he thought, as he sped along. "Anyway, we will have a roof over our heads and that is something. To be sure, the cottage is a poor one, but poor folks can't have everything as they want it."

When the boy arrived home he found his father had had another bad turn but was now resting easier. Without delay he told of what had happened at Deep Haven.

"Your aunt is a Tartar," said Louis Thompson. "I never liked her, and that is why I and your Uncle Peter have drifted apart. I thought he had sold the twelve-acre lot to Jerry Borden, who pastures his cows there."

"Jerry Borden will have to get out—that is, if we take possession," said Randy. "Mother, what do you think of it?"

"Is the cottage usable? I have not seen it for a year or more."

"It will have to be fixed up some. But I am sure I can do the work, with father's tools."

"It will save the rent money."

"And I can plant a garden, even if it is late. And we can keep some chickens, and then, after everything is in shape, I can again look for outside work."

"Randy's idea is a good one," answered the boy's father. "Our month will be up here next week. I'll notify the owner at once about leaving."

The next morning Randy went over to the twelve-acre farm, a corner of which sloped down to the river. He had passed it a hundred times before, but it was with an entirely different feeling that he surveyed it now.

It was pasture land, naturally good, but much neglected. A great many stones needed to be removed and the fences wanted propping up and here and there a new rail. The house, which faced a little side road, was a story and a half in height, with two rooms below and two chambers above. There was a well that needed fixing and also a cistern. Around the cottage the weeds grew high, and one of the windows was out and a door was missing.

"I can fix this place up, I am sure of it," said the boy to himself.

He was making a mental note of what was to be done when he heard a noise on the road and saw a farmer approaching, driving a dozen cows before him. It was Jerry Borden, the man who had been using the pasture lot without paying for it.

"Hullo! What air you a-doin' here?" asked Jerry Borden, looking at Randy in some surprise.

"We are going to move over here, Mr. Borden," answered Randy, calmly.

"Move over here!" ejaculated the farmer.

"Yes."

"In this air tumble-down cottage?"

"I am going to fix it up some."

"Well, I vow! It ain't fit to live in!"

"It will be."

"An' the land ain't wuth shucks."

"It seems to be good enough for the cows."

At this Jerry Borden's face fell a little.

"If you air a-goin' to move in, I guess thet means I'm to move out," he ventured.

"It does, unless——" Randy paused, stuck by a sudden idea.

"Unless what?" asked the farmer, eagerly. He wanted to use the lot very much, for he was short of pasturing on his own farm.

"Unless we can come to some sort of an agreement for milk and butter. Of course I can't let you use the whole lot, but you might use part of it."

"Did the owner say you could use the place?"

"Yes, we have it down in writing. We are to use it for five years and then we can buy it if we wish."

"I see." The farmer scratched his head. "Well, I dunno. Maybe we could let ye have butter an' milk. One thing is certain, I've got to have pasturin'."

"We could fence off part of the lot in some way, and you could use that."

"Thet's so."

"Besides that, I'll want some plowing done. I may have to hire you for that," pursued Randy.

"I must say I like your spunk, Randy. I shan't charge ye a cent fer plowin'."

After that the farmer and our hero talked matters over for half an hour, and the farmer told the youth what might be planted to advantage even so late in the season. Then Randy went home, feeling that the family was going to make a good move.

CHAPTER IX

THE NEW HOME

THE next few days were busy ones for Mrs. Thompson and for Randy. The landlord of the cottage in which they lived was notified that they were going to move, and then the woman set to work to get ready to vacate, while Randy went over to the other place to put the house in condition for occupancy.

While Randy was at work Jack came to see him, and insisted upon lending a helping hand. Randy had brought over some of his father's tools and also some nails, and he purchased at the lumber yard a few boards and other pieces he thought he needed.

When he once got at it, it was astonishing how well our hero used the tools, making several repairs that would have done credit to a regular carpenter. The broken window was replaced, and the missing door found and rehung, and several clapboards nailed fast. Then Randy mended the porch, and put a score of shingles on the roof. This done, the chimney was cleaned out and also the cistern, and the well was also overhauled. In the meantime Jack pulled out a lot of weeds and trained a wild honeysuckle over the porch. At the end of four days the place looked quite well.

"It's a hundred per cent. better than it was," declared Jack. "It didn't look like anything before."

"I'll get a can of paint to-morrow and paint the door and the window frames," said Randy, and this was done. He also whitewashed the kitchen, and kalsomined the other rooms, so that the interior of the cottage was sweet and clean.

When Mrs. Thompson saw the change which had been wrought she was delighted.

"I declare, it looks as well, if not better, than the cottage we are in," she cried. "And the outlook toward the river is ever so much nicer."

"Just wait until I have the garden in shape," said Randy. "You won't know the spot."

"What a pity we did not know of this place before."

"Mother, I think we ought to buy it if we can."

"Perhaps we shall, Randy, before the five years are up."

At length came the day to move. A local

truckman who knew Mr. Thompson well moved them for nothing.

"You can do some odd jobs for me some time," said the truckman to Louis Thompson.

"Thank you, I will—when I am able," answered the sufferer.

A good deal of the pain had left Mr. Thompson, but he was weak, and to start to regular work was out of the question. Another friend took him to his new cottage in a carriage. He gazed at the old place in wonder.

"Well, it certainly is improved!" he ejaculated. "We shall get along here very well."

The moving was done early in the morning and by nightfall Randy and his mother had the cottage in tolerable order. The stove was set up and found to draw good, and the water from the well tasted fine.

"Now there is one thing certain," said Randy, "Mother, come what may, we shall have a roof over our heads."

"Yes, my son, and I am grateful for it," answered Mrs. Thompson.

"Uncle Peter may be a hard man to get along with, but he has certainly helped us."

The next two weeks were busy ones for Randy. Jerry Borden was true to his promise and not only did some plowing for the Thompsons but also helped Randy to put up a new fence, partly of stone and partly of rails. It was agreed that Borden should have the use of part of the little farm for pasturing, and in return was to give the Thompsons two quarts of milk a day and two pounds of butter per week, and also a dozen fresh eggs a week while the hens were laying.

"That will certainly help us out wonderfully," said Mrs. Thompson. "Butter, eggs, and milk are quite an item of expense."

"And that is not all," said Randy. "I am going to help Mr. Borden with his haying soon and he is going to pay us in early vegetables."

The haying time was already at hand, and Randy soon pitched in with a will, much to his neighbor's satisfaction.

One day Jack came to bring good news. His father had secured a position with an iron works at Albany, on the Hudson River.

"It will pay him a fair salary," said Jack.

"I am glad to hear it," answered Randy. "What will your family do, remain here or move to Albany?"

"We are going to remain here for the present, but, if the place suits father after he has been there a while, then we'll move."

"Have you learned anything more about the Bangses?"

"Mrs. Bangs and Bob are on a summer vacation."

"Yes, I know that. I meant Mr. Bangs."

"He is in full charge at the iron works here and drawing a salary of eight thousand dollars a year. Father says he will run the works into the ground so that the stock won't be worth a cent."

"Can't your father do anything?"

"Not yet. But he is going to watch things. There was some trouble over a contract and he is trying to get to the bottom of that," continued Jack.

When Randy went to work for Farmer Borden he came into contact with the farmer's son Sammy, a tall, overgrown lad of fourteen, with a freckled face and a shock of red hair. Sammy hated to work, and his father and mother had to fairly drive him to get anything out of him.

"City folks don't work like farmers," remarked Sammy to Randy. "They jest lay off an' take it easy."

"How do you know that?" asked our hero, in quiet amusement.

"'Cos I once read a paper of the sports in the city."

"Some rich folks don't work, Sammy. But all the others work as hard as we do."

"I don't believe it," said Sammy, stoutly. "Wish I was a city lad. Oh, wouldn't I jest have the bang-up time, though!"

"Sammy Borden!" cried his mother, shrilly. "You get to work, an' be quick about it."

"I'm tired," answered the freckled-faced lad.

"Tired? Lazy, you mean! Git to work, or I'll have your paw give you a dressin' down!"

"Drat the luck!" muttered Sammy, as he took up his pitchfork. "I wish I was born in the city!"

"Come on, Sammy," said Randy. "The work has got to be done, so don't think about it, but do it."

"Huh! Work is easy to you, Randy Thompson! But it comes hard on me!" And Sammy heaved a ponderous sigh.

The haying was in full blast early in July and Randy worked early and late. He wanted to get through, so that he might go at his own garden. Sammy dragged worse than ever, and finally confided to our hero that he wanted to go to the city over the Fourth.

"Have you asked your folks yet?" asked Randy.

"No, but I'm a-goin' to," answered Sammy.

"Well, if you go, I hope you have a good time," said our hero. "I'd like to see a Fourth of July in the city myself. I've heard they make a good deal of noise, but I shouldn't mind that."

"Gosh! I love shootin'," said Sammy.

"Aren't you afraid you might get lost?" pursued Randy.

"Lost!" snorted Sammy. "Not much! Why, you can't lose me in the woods, much less in the city."

"The city and the woods are two different places."

"I don't care. I'd know what I was doin'."

"It costs money to go to the city."

"I want to go to Springfield."

"Have you any money saved up?"

To this Sammy did not answer. Then Mr. Borden came along.

"Sammy, get to work!" he called out. "Don't let Randy do everything."

"I was workin'," grumbled the son, as he started in again. "You can't expect a feller like me to pitch hay all day long."

"I have to work all day," retorted his father.

"It ain't fair nohow."

"If you want to eat you'll have to work."

Sammy pitched in, but grumbled a good deal to himself. Soon his mother called him and he went off to the house.

"That lad is gettin' lazier every day," said Jerry Borden. "I declare, I don't know what to do with him."

"Maybe he needs a vacation," suggested our hero.

"Well, he can't have one until the hayin' is done," declared the farmer.

CHAPTER X

SAMMY'S FOURTH OF JULY

THE next day Sammy sat on a bench on the cottage stoop, apparently very intent on a perusal of the Farmer's Almanac, but it was evident his thoughts were somewhere else.

"What in nater is the boy a-doin'?" asked his mother, looking up from a pile of stockings she was mending. "If he ain't twisting up thet Almanac as if 'twasn't any more than a piece of brown paper. What are you thinking about, Sammy?"

"Thursday is Fourth o' July," answered her son.

"Well, what if it is? I'm sure I'm willing."

"They are going to have great doings down to Springfield," added Sammy.

"Is that so? I hope they enjoy themselves. But it ain't anything to me as I know on."

"I want to go down an' see the celebration," said Sammy, mustering up his courage to give utterance to so daring a proposition.

"Want to see the Fourth o' July in Springfield?" ejaculated his mother. "Is the boy crazy? Ain't it the Fourth o' July here as well as there, I'd like to know?"

"Well, I suppose it is, but I never was in Springfield, an' I want to go. They've got a lot o' shows there, an' I'm bound to see some on 'em."

"Sammy," said his mother, solemnly, "it would be the ruination of you; you'd git shot, or something wuss. You ain't nuthin' but a boy, an' couldn't be trusted nohow."

"Ain't I fourteen, an' ain't I 'most six feet high?" answered back Sammy, defiantly. "An' didn't Dick Slade, who is only thirteen, go down last Fourth an' have a smashin' good time an' not git hurt?"

"But you ain't got no experience, Sammy."

"I've got enough to go to Springfield."

"No, you had better give up the notion."

"Now, mother, don't say that!" pleaded the son.

"But I do say it."

"Well, then I'm going to—to run away! I'll go to sea an' be a sailor, or sumthin'!" burst out Sammy, recklessly. "I'm sick o' workin' every single day!"

"Stop talking in that dreadful way, Sammy!" said Mrs. Borden, anxiously.

"Then you ask paw to let me go."

"'Twon't do no good."

"Yes, it will. You ask him, won't you?" pleaded the son.

At last Mrs. Borden consented and spoke to her husband about it during the dinner hour. Jerry Borden shook his head.

"He can't go—it's sheer foolishness," he said.

"If you don't let him go I'm afraid he will run away," said the wife. "He has his heart set on going." Sammy was out of the room at the time, so he could not hear the talk.

At first Mr. Borden would not listen, but at last he gave in, although he added grimly that he thought running away would do Sammy a world of good.

"He'd be mighty glad to sneak back afore a week was up," he said.

When Sammy realized that he was really to go to the city he was wild with delight, and rushed down into the hayfield to tell Randy of his plans.

"I'm a-goin' to have a highfalutin' time," he said. "Just you wait until I come back an' tell about it."

"I hope you do have a good time," answered our hero, "and don't get hurt."

"There won't nothin' happen to me," answered Sammy, confidently.

Early on the morning of Independence Day Sammy stood at the door of the farmhouse arrayed in his Sunday best. His folks were there to see him off.

"My son," said Mr. Borden, "don't ye be wasteful o' your money, an' don't git in no scrapes."

"An' remember, Sammy, to keep all the Commandments," added his mother, as she kissed him tenderly.

Soon he was off, down the side road towards the highway, where the stage passed that ran to the railroad station. His walk took him by the Thompson cottage. Randy was at home and fixing up the garden.

"I'm off!" yelled Sammy, waving his hand.

"Good luck!" cried Randy, pleasantly. "Don't get your head shot off."

"He may lose his head without having it shot off," remarked Mr. Thompson, who sat on the porch, with his rheumatic side in the sunshine.

"I do not think it very wise to let him go to the

city alone," put in Mrs. Thompson from the kitchen.

Sammy tramped on until he came to the main highway and there waited impatiently for the stage to appear. He got a seat by the driver, and in less than an hour reached the railroad station. He had been on the cars before, yet the ride was much of a novelty.

At last the country boy found himself on the streets of Springfield. There was an extra celebration of some sort going on and great crowds flocked on every side. Poor Sammy was completely bewildered, as he was jostled first one way and then another.

"Well, by gosh! If this don't beat anything I ever see!" he ejaculated. "Where in thunder did all the folks come from, anyway?"

Sammy looked so truly rural that he attracted the attention of two street urchins who were standing close by.

"There's a greeny, I'll bet a hat!" said one of them, nudging his companion.

"A regular one and no mistake," answered the second urchin.

"Let's have a little fun out of him."

"How?"

"Just look and you'll see how I fix him."

So speaking, he took a bunch of firecrackers from his pocket and, with a pin, attached it to the tail of Sammy's coat. Then he set the bunch on fire and slipped back into the crowd.

Crack! Crack! Bang!

The plot took effect. Sammy was aroused from his reverie by explosion after explosion in his immediate rear. He started and leaped into the air in wild amazement.

"By thunder!" he gasped. "Is thet a cannon bustin'?"

The crackers continued to go off, and poor Sammy leaped around worse than ever.

"Say, mister, what's up?" he asked of a man who was laughing loudly.

"Look behind you," answered the man.

Sammy did so. One look was enough. He began to bellow like a bull and started off on a run, knocking down several people who happened to be in his way. At last a police officer stopped him.

"What do you mean by making such a disturbance?" demanded the officer.

"I'm burning up! I'm exploding! Don't you hear me?" gasped poor Sammy.

"Pooh! It's only fire-crackers," and the policeman smiled faintly.

"Take 'em off, mister, please do!" pleaded Sammy. "I'll give you ten cents for the job!"

"They are about burned out," answered the officer, as the last firecracker went off with an extra loud bang. "You are safe. Go along with you." And he waved his stick. Sammy lost no time in sneaking off. The boy who had played the trick had a good laugh and so did his companion.

Soon Sammy heard a band and saw some "Milingtary," as he called them, approaching. The sight of the soldiers with their guns awed him, yet he followed the procession to a grove, where there was more music and also speechmaking. He listened to the orations with wide-open mouth, until he suddenly lost interest when a bit of banana skin was thrown at him, landing directly in the opening.

"Wah!" he spluttered. "Who threw thet skin at me?"

He could not find the offender and so roamed around the grove, presently halting before a temporary stand filled with things to eat. He now discovered that he was tremendously hungry.

"Snathers take the expense," he muttered to himself. "I'm a-goin' to have something to eat if it breaks me." He had brought along a lunch from home, but had forgotten it on the train.

He approached the stand and looked the stock of eatables over.

"What's the price o' them bananas, mister?" he asked.

"Two cents each."

"Well, I suppose if I take two you'll let me have 'em fer three cents."

"Couldn't do it."

"Well, who cares, anyway? It's only four cents. Let me have two."

The bananas were handed over and Sammy looked for his change. But he only had two cents and a one-dollar bill.

"Can you change that?" he asked, holding out the bill.

"Certainly," answered the standkeeper, and promptly gave the youth a fifty-cent piece and a lot of small change. With his bananas in one hand and his money in another Sammy retired to a distance, to count his change and make sure it was right.

While he was buying the fruit a boy in tatters watched him eagerly. Now the boy came up to the country lad.

"Please, mister, won't you give me some money

to buy bread with?" he asked, in a quivering voice.

"To buy bread with?" asked Sammy, in astonishment.

"Yes, please—I'm awful hungry."

"Ain't you had nuthin' to eat to-day?"

"Not a mouthful."

Sammy's compassion was aroused and he began to look over his change.

"Look out for that!" cried the tattered boy, looking upward suddenly.

Sammy's gaze traveled in the same direction. As his eyes went up the boy in rags grabbed the money in his hand and in an instant was making off through the crowd.

The movement was so quick, and the surprise so great, that for the moment Sammy was bereft of speech.

At length he recovered sufficiently to shout the single word at the top of his lungs:

"Constable!"

"What's the matter?" asked a policeman, running up.

"Thief! Robbery!"

"Where is the thief?"

"He ran off."

"Where? In what direction?"

"I—er—I don't know," stammered Sammy.

"What did he take?"

"Took all my money."

"How much?"

"Ninety-six cents. It ain't all—I've got two cents left."

"Well, if you can point out the thief I'll arrest him," said the policeman. "Come, we'll take a look around."

This was done, but the boy in rags could not be found.

"Drat the luck! I suppose the money is gone fer good!" groaned Sammy, and he was right. For he never saw either the boy or his cash again.

Sammy had expected to remain in the evening and see the fire-works, but now his interest in the celebration was gone.

"Hain't got but two cents left!" he groaned. "Thet won't buy no supper nor nuthin! It's lucky I've got a train ticket back. But I'll have to walk to hum from the station, unless they'll tick me fer the stage ride."

He walked around, still hoping to meet the lad who had robbed him. His perambulations presently brought him to a spot where there was a pond of water, in which some gold-fish were swimming. The gold-fish caught his eye and he paused to watch them as they darted about.

He was leaning over, looking into the pond, when some boys came along on a run. One boy shoved another and he fell up against Sammy. As a consequence the country lad lost his balance and went into the pond with a loud splash.

"Save me!" he spluttered. "I can't swim!"

"Wade out; it's only up to your middle!" sang out a man, and arising, Sammy did as directed. He was covered with mud and slime and presented anything but a nice appearance.

"This is the wust yet!" he muttered, and felt half like crying. "I ain't going to stay here no more—I'm goin' straight fer hum!"

CHAPTER XI

RANDY TO THE RESCUE

THE next day Randy went over to the Borden farm to finish up his work there. To his astonishment Sammy was on hand and apparently eager to go to work.

"Well, how was the celebration, Sammy?" asked our hero.

"No good."

"That's too bad."

"After this I'm a-goin' to stay to hum on the Fourth," went on Sammy, as he began to fork over the hay vigorously. "I ain't goin' to no city to be skinned."

"Did they skin you?"

"Jest about. A feller robbed me an' I was pushed into a duck pond."

"That's too bad."

"If I hadn't a-had my train ticket I'd had to walk home," went on Sammy. "As it was, I had to borrow fifteen cents on the stage, to pay fer thet ride. No more city celebrations fer me. I kin have all I want right here at Riverport." And then Sammy related his adventures in detail, to which our hero listened with much secret amusement.

Over at the Thompson place the ground had been plowed up in part, and as soon as he left Jerry Borden Randy set to work in earnest to plant late vegetables. For what our hero had done for the Bordens he was paid in vegetables, and also received a rooster and four hens. This gave the Thompsons their own eggs, for which the lady of the cottage was thankful.

Randy was at work early one morning, when Jack appeared.

"Hullo, at it already?" sang out Jack. "I thought I'd find you still in bed."

"I prefer to work when the sun is not so hot," answered Randy. "But what brings you out at such an hour as this?"

"I've got news."

"What is it?"

"We are going to move to Albany."

"When?"

"The first of next week."

"I'll be sorry to miss you, Jack."

"And I'll be sorry to leave you, Randy. But

I came over for something more than to tell the news. I want you to go fishing with me. They say the sport is extra fine just now."

"I don't know if I can go," answered our hero, doubtfully. "There is still enough to do here."

"It will be a change for you. You have worked very hard lately."

"I admit that."

"Go by all means, if you care to, Randy," called out Mrs. Thompson. "You have earned a holiday, and the fish will be acceptable."

"All right, mother; if you say so, I'll go."

It did not take Randy long to prepare for the outing. Jack had with him a basket of lunch for two, so all he had to get was his line and hooks and some extra bait.

"I hope we catch a good mess to-day," said Randy, as they started off. "Then I can give Mr. Borden some and he can let us have some bacon that we need."

"I suppose it is rather hard scratching for you just now," said Jack.

"It is, and I am going to look for outside work before long."

"Well, I hope you find something to do. Ben Bash was looking for work all over this district but he couldn't find a thing."

"Oh, I know there is small chance in Riverport. I think I may try elsewhere," answered our hero.

It did not take the two boys long to reach the river, at a point where Jack had left his boat. Both rowed to their favorite fishing spot.

"Oh, isn't that too bad!" cried Jack, in disappointment.

Strangers were fishing at the spot and they soon saw that there was no room for them to throw in.

"How is fishing?" called out Randy.

"Very good," answered one of those present.

"We'll have to go elsewhere," said Jack. "The question is, where?"

"I know another spot about quarter of a mile from here," answered Randy. "It may be just as good."

They rowed on and reached the new place, to find nobody there. Soon they had their boat tied fast to an overhanging tree and then they got out on some flat rocks and baited up.

It did not take long to prove that the new fishing place was as good as the old. Randy drew in a small fish almost immediately and Jack did the same. Then both got hauls of good size.

"Maybe we'll do better than if we went to the old Fishing Hole," observed Jack.

At noon time they knocked off for lunch and a rest and then took a good swim.

"I can tell you, I enjoy this!" cried Randy. "I haven't had a chance to go in for so long."

The swim at an end, the boys donned their garments and resumed their fishing. They kept at it until about four o'clock. Then all their luck seemed to suddenly desert them.

"Never mind," said Randy. "We certainly have a prime haul, even as it is," and he looked the fish over with much pride.

They wound up their lines and were soon on the way down the river. It was rather a hot day, so they took their time in getting back.

"What are you going to do with your boat?" asked Randy.

"Sell it to Mr. Stanwood for ten dollars."

"You are lucky to get a customer, Jack."

"I know it. I'd turn the boat over to you only—well—we need the money now, you know," and Jack's eyes dropped.

"Thank you, Jack, but I wouldn't have much time to use it. I must put in the most of my time at work."

"I suppose that is true. At the same time I'd rather you had the boat than anybody I know of."

The boys were coming around a bend of the river when they heard a peculiar noise in the distance.

"What do you make that out to be?" asked Jack, as the noise continued.

"I think I know," answered our hero. "It is the new tugboat from the bay. I saw it once, several weeks ago. It makes a very odd sound, for the engine is not like the ordinary ones."

The noise kept coming closer and presently the tugboat came into view. It was stuck in the mud and those on board were doing what they could to get the craft afloat again.

"They seem to be having a hard time of it," remarked Jack, as he stopped rowing to watch the proceedings.

"The mud is very sticky here, if you'll remember," answered Randy. "Don't you remember how we were stuck here last year?"

"Yes, and how I lost an oar overboard and nearly went overboard myself," continued Jack, with a short laugh. "Heigh-ho! Randy, I'll be sorry in a way to lose it all."

"We must write to each other."

"Of course."

The tug was puffing and snorting viciously to

get out of the mud. On board were four people who were evidently passengers, including a lady with a little girl.

Suddenly there came something which sounded like an explosion. This was followed by a cloud of steam that seemed to completely envelop the tugboat.

"Something is wrong!" shouted Randy.

"Oh, mamma, I don't like this!" screamed the little girl, as she ran to the stern of the tug. "We'll be burned up!"

She had scarcely spoken when there came another explosion and the cloud of steam increased. The four passengers crowded to the stern in a body, and a moment later the two men leaped overboard and called on the lady and her child to do likewise.

"I cannot swim!" shrieked the lady.

"You must jump!" answered somebody. "The tug may blow up!"

The little girl heard this and with a scream she ran from her mother straight for the bow of the tug. The next moment she lost her balance and went overboard.

"She's over!" cried Randy, and his heart leaped into his throat.

"Save my child! Save Helen!" shrieked the

lady and rushed after her offspring. Soon she was in the water also.

The situation was certainly a thrilling one. The two men in the water were fifty feet away and those left on the tug were in no position to render assistance. The child had disappeared completely, while the mother was thrashing around wildly, in water just up to her neck.

"Quick, Jack, turn the boat around!" ejaculated Randy. "We must get them on board."

The craft was turned around and headed for the lady. Then Randy threw off his cap—he was already in his shirt sleeves—and stood up in the bow. He gazed anxiously into the muddy water and caught a dim view of the little girl's white dress.

"My child! My child!" the mother continued to scream.

"I'll bring her up," said Randy, and made a leap overboard, just as the gunwale of the row-boat came within reaching distance of the lady's hands.

The little girl had been caught by the current and was being carried down the stream. Randy made a quick grab but missed her, and then she disappeared from view. But in a few seconds more he saw her again, and this time secured hold

"SHE'S OVER!" CRIED RANDY.—P. 105.

Randy of the River

of her arm. The next moment he raised her to the surface of the river.

She was too far gone to do anything but splutter. She clutched him with a deathlike grip—a thing every person in danger of drowning will do—and he had his hands full to keep both himself and his burden afloat. Shallow water was not far off and he struck out for this and waded ashore.

In the meantime Jack was having no easy time of it getting the lady into the rowboat. There was serious danger of the craft overturning, and he had to caution her to be careful.

"My child! My Helen!" she moaned, when she was at last safe.

"My friend will save her," answered Jack.

"You are sure?"

"Yes."

CHAPTER XII

A STEAMBOAT MAN

HAVING saved the lady from her uncomfortable if not dangerous position, Jack lost no time in rowing for the shore. Soon he was at the river bank and the lady leaped out of the rowboat and ran to where Randy had placed his dripping burden on the grass.

"My Helen! Is she safe?" asked the lady, anxiously.

"I think so," answered our hero. "But I guess she swallowed some river water."

"Oh, how thankful I am that you went after her."

"It was the only thing to do. I saw she couldn't swim."

The little girl was still gasping for breath. The mother threw herself on the grass and did what she could for her. Soon the little girl gave a cry:

"Mamma!"

"Yes, darling, I am here!"

"Oh, dear! I am all wet!"

"Be thankful that your life has been spared."

"That boy brought me out of the water."

"Yes, dear—and he was brave to do it," answered the mother and beamed on Randy to such an extent that he had to blush.

By this time the two men had also come ashore. The steam was still blowing off on the tug but the danger appeared to be over. Later the engineer announced that a valve and a connection had broken, and the craft would have to remain where she was until towed off.

"I am glad to see you are all safe," said the man who ran the tug. "There wasn't very much danger on board."

"It looked bad enough," said one of the men who had leaped overboard. "I didn't want to get scalded."

"And neither did I," added the other.

It appeared that neither of the men knew the lady excepting by name. She was, however, fairly well known to the tug captain, and had gone up the river on the craft to please her little girl.

"I am sorry for this, Mrs. Shalley," said the tug owner. "I must say, I don't know what to do."

"I must get dry clothing on Helen pretty soon."

"The tug is wet from end to end from the escaped steam."

"If I was down at Riverport I could go to the hotel," went on Mrs. Shalley.

"We can take you down in our rowboat," said Jack. "It won't take very long."

"Can I trust myself in the boat?"

"Certainly, if you'll only sit still."

The matter was talked over, and it was decided that the lady and her little girl should be taken down to Riverport by Randy and Jack. The party was soon on the way.

"My name is Mrs. Andrew Shalley," said the lady. "My husband is a steamboat owner. May I ask your names?"

"Mine is Jack Bartlett. I live in Riverport, but I am going to move to Albany."

"And my name is Randy Thompson," added our hero. "I live over there—in the little cottage by that clump of trees."

"I am pleased to know you," said the lady. "It was more than kind of both of you to come to the assistance of myself and my daughter."

"It wasn't so much to do," answered Randy. "We were close by."

"You are soaking wet."

"It's an old working suit and I don't mind the water," laughed our hero.

"What a nice lot of fish," said little Helen, who had now completely recovered.

"I feel I should reward you both," went on Mrs. Shalley.

"I don't want anything," said Jack, promptly.

"And neither do I," added our hero.

The hotel at which the lady was stopping was built close to the river bank. Mother and child landed at the dock and Randy and Jack bade them good-by.

"I shall try to see you again," said Mrs. Shalley, as she started for the hotel.

"Evidently a very nice lady," remarked Jack, as he and Randy rowed away.

"Yes."

"I think she wanted to reward us, Randy."

"I think so myself, but I don't want any reward."

"Neither do I, although I shouldn't mind, say ten thousand dollars," went on Jack, by way of a joke.

"Or the Presidency of the United States," added Randy, in an equally light tone.

The boys had caught so many fish Randy decided to sell some from his share. He found a purchaser on the dock where they landed and started home richer by fifty cents.

"If I can't get anything else to do, I can do some fishing later on," he mused. "I can get at least two or three dollars' worth of fish a week, and that would be better than nothing—and I could keep right on with the farm, too."

When Randy returned home he had quite a story to tell, to which both his father and his mother listened with interest.

"Randy, you must be careful in the water," said Mrs. Thompson, with an anxious look in her eyes. "Supposing that girl had dragged you down?"

"I was on my guard, mother."

"Randy is a good swimmer," said his father. "I was a good swimmer myself, in my younger days."

The fish proved acceptable, and Randy readily got Jerry Borden to trade him some bacon for a mess, and also give him some fresh vegetables.

"Gosh! Wish I'd gone fishing," said Sammy. "I like to catch big fish."

"Well, I am not going to stop you," said our hero.

"Sammy never has no luck," put in Mrs. Borden. "Once he went fishing all day and all he got was three little fish."

"Didn't nuther!" cried Sammy. "I got twelve big bites, but they got away."

"It's the big fish that always get away," said Randy, with a smile. "Never mind, Sammy, maybe we can go together some day."

"I'd like that," answered the overgrown country boy.

"Did that Bartlett boy get any fish?" asked Mrs. Borden.

"Just as many as I did."

"I understand they are going to move away."

"Yes, to Albany."

"They say down to the iron works that Mr. Bangs is glad to have Mr. Bartlett out of the place."

"I guess that is true."

"It's too bad! All of the men liked Mr. Bartlett."

"Don't they like Mr. Bangs?"

"Not a bit—so Mr. Reilly was telling my husband. They say Mr. Bangs is mean to everybody."

Two days slipped by, and Randy was at work in the garden one afternoon when he saw a buggy stop at the front of the cottage and a portly man alighted. Knowing his mother was busy, our hero went to meet the newcomer.

"Is this where Randy Thompson lives?" asked the portly gentleman.

"Yes, sir, I am Randy Thompson."

"Oh!" The gentleman held out his hand. "I am glad to know you. "My name is Andrew Shalley. You did my wife and little girl a great service the other day."

"I only did what seemed necessary," answered Randy, modestly. "Will you come into the house, Mr. Shalley?"

"Thanks, I'll sit down on your porch." The gentleman did so. "What are you doing, farming?"

"A little. We got this place so late this season I cannot do a great deal. Next year I hope to have the farm in much better shape."

"Do you like it?"

"I try to like it."

"Then you are not naturally a farmer?"

"No, sir."

"Is your father living?"

"Yes, sir; but he is laid up with rheumatism, so he cannot work at present. He is a carpenter."

"Indeed! I was a carpenter when I was a young man."

"I thought Mrs. Shalley said you were a steamboat owner."

"I am, now. I gave up carpentering to go into the freight business. I made money, and then bought a small freight boat. Then I branched out, and now own a steamboat running up and down the Hudson River, and I also own several steam tugs."

"Do you own the one that got into trouble the other day?"

"No, a friend of mine owns that—that is how my wife and little girl happened to be on board. I am——" Mr. Shalley stopped short as a form appeared in the doorway behind him.

"This is my mother. Mother, this is Mr. Shalley, the steamboat owner."

"I am glad to meet you," said Mrs. Thompson, politely. "Will you come in?"

"Thank you, but it is very pleasant on the porch. Madam, you have a good son," went on the steamboat owner.

"I know that."

"He did my wife and little girl a great service the other day."

"Yes, he told me what he did."

"I think—er—that is, I'd like to reward you," stammered Andrew Shalley. He saw that Randy was no common boy with whom to deal.

"Thank you, but I don't wish any reward, sir."

"I felt you would say that," answered Andrew Shalley. "The other lad said the same."

"Then you have seen Jack Bartlett?"

"Yes, I just came from there. I wanted to reward him, but he would not have it. But I fixed him," and the steamboat owner smiled broadly.

"Yes?" said Mrs. Thompson, curiously.

"I found out he was going to move to Albany, so I gave him a free pass on my steamboat, the *Helen Shalley*—named after my wife. Now he can go up and down the river as much as he pleases and it won't cost him a cent. I told him I'd depend upon him to haul folks out of the water if they fell overboard," and the steamboat owner laughed broadly.

"That ought to suit Jack—he loves the water so," said Randy.

"Do you like the water, too?"

"Yes, sir."

"Then maybe you'd like a pass also."

"I couldn't use it, Mr. Shalley."

"I was only joking. But really, Randy, I'd like to do something for you, to show I appreciate what you did for my wife and for Helen."

"I do not want anything, Mr. Shalley, excepting work."

"Work? I should imagine you had enough of that right here."

"I mean work that would pay me regular wages. We must have money. My father needs the doctor, and medicine, and we have to buy groceries, and such, and we can't make the farm pay the bills."

"I understand, my lad. Where is your father?"

"I am here, sir," came from the couch in the sitting room.

"May I come in, Mr. Thompson?"

"Certainly," answered the sick man, and a moment later Andrew Shalley entered the cottage and was shaking hands with Randy's father.

CHAPTER XIII

MR. SHALLEY MAKES AN OFFER

THE two men conversed together for fully half an hour, and during that time Andrew Shalley learned much concerning the Thompson family and their struggle to make both ends meet.

"I live at Nyack," said Andrew Shalley. "And my headquarters for boats is there also. But the passenger steamer runs from New York City to Albany. The tugs run anywhere on the river and on New York Bay."

"It must be a nice business," said Randy. "I like boats of any kind."

"If I had a boat on the river here I might give you a job," went on the gentleman. "But all of my craft are on the Hudson."

"They tell me that the Hudson is a grand stream."

"Nothing finer in this country, my boy, nothing finer. I have traveled all over the United States and I know. I think it is fully equal to the German Rhine and the St. Lawrence."

"Maybe you could give me a situation on one of your Hudson River boats," went on Randy, struck by a sudden idea.

"Would you care to leave home?"

"Oh, Randy, you wouldn't want to go away!" cried Mrs. Thompson.

"I would if it paid to do so," answered Randy, quickly. "There isn't much chance for work in Riverport."

"And I can keep an eye on the garden," said Mr. Thompson. "I know I am going to feel some better now this spell is passing."

"If you cared to leave home I might give you some sort of a job on one of my boats," went on Andrew Shalley, thoughtfully.

"What kind of a job?"

"I'd have to see about it first. I'll tell you what I'll do, I'll send you a letter next week."

"Thank you."

"That will be best. But now I am going to do something else." The steamboat man drew out his wallet. "I want you to accept this." And he held out five crisp ten-dollar bills.

Randy did not wish to take the money, but the steamboat man urged it and finally laid the bills on the table.

"I am sure you are more than kind, Mr. Shalley," said Mrs. Thompson. "I shall remember you."

"Let us call it a loan," said Mr. Thompson, "to be paid back when I am at work once more."

"Yes, call it a loan," said Randy, "otherwise I, for one, don't want it."

"Have your way," laughed Mr. Shalley. "But don't worry about the payment."

Before he left he walked around the little farm and praised what Randy had done.

"Evidently not a lazy boy," he told himself, "and one who is willing to aid his parents. That is the sort I like."

"He is a very nice man," said Mrs. Thompson, when the visitor had departed. "Randy, you were fortunate to make such a friend."

"Yes. But, mother, I think we ought to pay back that money some day."

"I can do that—when I am able to go at carpentering again," put in Mr. Thompson.

After that a week passed quietly enough. Randy worked early and late and got the little farm in good shape and also visited Jack and bade his friend good-by.

"Maybe I'll get a position on one of the Hudson River boats," said our hero.

"If you do, and you stop at Albany, you must

come and see me," answered Jack, and gave his new address.

On the following Monday came a letter from Andrew Shalley. It was short and to the point and read in part as follows:

"All I can offer you at present is the position of a deckhand on my steamboat, the *Helen Shalley.* If you wish to accept that I will pay you twenty dollars per month and your board at the start, and more when you are experienced. If you wish to accept, write to me and come on to Nyack, to my office."

"Here's an offer at last!" cried Randy, as he read the communication. He had been fearful that Andrew Shalley might forget him.

"Twenty dollars per month is not so very much," said his mother.

"Yes, but I am to get my board, so the money will all be clear profit, outside of the cost of my clothing."

"I suppose you will live on the boat," put in Mr. Thompson. "Most of the crew do."

"I can send the most of the money home each month," continued Randy.

"The boat won't run during the winter," said

his mother, who did not much relish having her son leave home.

"Well, it will run until cold weather, anyway, and perhaps after that Mr. Shalley will give me something else to do."

The matter was discussed that evening, and before he retired, Randy penned a letter to the steamboat owner, stating he would come to Nyack two days later.

The prospects ahead filled our hero with pleasure. The new position would enable him to see a little of the world and meet other people, and he was sure steamboat life would suit him thoroughly. He knew there would be plenty of hard work, handling freight and baggage, but this did not daunt him.

"I'll try to do my best," he reasoned. "Then maybe Mr. Shalley will give me something better later on."

Randy did not have many clothes, so there was not a great deal to pack. What he possessed was gone over by his mother, and then packed in a valise. Out of the money on hand he was given the price of his stage and railroad ticket and five dollars for other expenses.

"I shan't spend only what is necessary," said he to his parents.

Randy was glad to see that his father was improving. A good deal of the rheumatic pains had left Mr. Thompson and he could get around the house and the garden. It would be some time before he could go at carpentering again, but he could aid a good deal on the farm, which was something.

All too soon for his mother came the time for Randy to depart. Mrs. Thompson kissed him affectionately and his father shook him by the hand.

"Come back home if it doesn't suit you, Randy," said the mother.

"Yes, come back, and we'll get along somehow," added his father.

"I am sure it will suit me," said the boy. "I know the kind of a man Mr. Shalley is. We'll be sure to get along."

Randy left home early in the morning and half an hour later was on the stage, bound for Leeville, where he was to take the train for Tarrytown, which is directly across the Hudson River from Nyack. His going away was done so quietly that not a dozen persons knew of his departure. The stage was but half filled, so he had plenty of room both for himself and his valise.

Arriving at Leeville he had an hour to wait for

the train and spent the time in walking around the little town.

He had just passed one of the largest stores when he felt a hand on his shoulder and turned, to find himself confronted by Bob Bangs.

"What are you doing here?" demanded the big boy, rather impudently.

"What business is that of yours?" retorted Randy, not liking the manner in which he had been addressed.

"Oh, you needn't answer if you don't want to," sniffed Bob Bangs.

"I am going to Nyack."

"To Nyack? What for?"

"I am going to work for a steamboat owner."

"Humph! Going to work on the river?"

"Yes."

"Cabin boy, I suppose," sneered the rich boy.

"No, as a deckhand."

"I thought so. It's a dirty enough job, and you are welcome to it."

"It's honest work, and the money is clean," answered Randy, warmly.

"Ha! What do you mean by clean money," demanded the big boy, suspiciously.

"Just what I said."

"Maybe you are trying to help spread that report that the Bartletts started about us," said the rich youth.

"What report do you mean, Bob?"

"You know well enough—the one about my father."

"I don't know."

"Ain't the Bartletts telling everybody that my father shoved 'em out of the iron works and that our money wasn't clean?"

"I haven't heard it."

"Bah! You needn't play the innocent. I know you, and I know Jack Bartlett, too."

"I don't think your folks treated the Bartletts just right," went on our hero, resolved to stand up for his friends.

"We treated 'em better than they deserved. If I had been my father I should have kicked old man Bartlett out."

"Your father wouldn't have dared, Bob Bangs. But I am not going to quarrel with you. What brings you to this place?"

"That's my business."

"You needn't tell me if you don't wish to."

"I am here to get a new horse. I am going to ride horseback after this," went on the rich boy, boastfully. "It's a horse that costs four hundred dollars, too."

"Then you are in luck," was all Randy answered, and walked away, leaving the rich youth gazing after him doubtfully.

CHAPTER XIV

BOB BANGS AND HIS HORSE

Randy continued to wander around the country town, taking in such sights as came to view.

In the meantime Bob Bangs went after the horse he had mentioned. The rich youth had bothered his father for a horse for a long time and at last Mr. Bangs had consented to give him a steed. The horse was to be taken in exchange for a debt, and Bob had agreed to go to Leeville after him and take the animal to the summer resort at which he and his mother were stopping. It may be mentioned that the horse was worth only a hundred and fifty dollars, but the falsehood he had told in regard to the horse's value did not bother Bob Bangs in the least. He loved to boast upon every possible occasion.

"Is he gentle?" asked the rich boy, as he approached the horse, that was standing in the yard of the former owner.

"As gentle as a lamb," was the answer.

"He—he won't run away, will he?" went on Bob, timidly. To tell the truth he knew very little about horses, although he pretended to know a great deal.

"He never ran away in his life," declared the man who was disposing of the horse.

"Then I guess it is all right," said the rich boy, and started to mount into the saddle, for the steed was ready for use.

"Wait a minute."

"What's wanted now."

"I want you to sign a receipt first," said the man.

"Oh, all right."

The receipt was produced, stating that the horse was received in good condition and that the debt was canceled thereby, and the rich youth signed his father's name and his own under it. Then the man held the horse while the boy mounted.

"All safe and sound?" asked the man.

"Yes," answered Bob Bangs. "Good-day," and off he rode.

"Good-day, and good luck to you," answered the man, and he smiled rather grimly to himself as he entered his house.

"The horse seems to be a nice one," thought Bob Bangs, as he rode away. "I wish I could meet Randy Thompson, it would make him feel sick to see me on such a fine animal."

The rich youth's wish was gratified, for turning a corner he caught sight of our hero just as the latter was crossing the street.

"Out of the way there, Randy Thompson!" he cried, and urged his horse forward.

Randy had to jump back, or he might have been knocked down.

"Ain't this a fine horse?" Bob Bangs cried. "Don't you wish you had him?"

And he cut the steed with the whip he carried, to make him increase his speed.

The horse did not like the treatment received and up came his hind hoofs viciously.

"Stop! None of that!" roared Bob Bangs, in fright. "Whoa there!"

He began to saw on the reins, and as a consequence the horse turned first in one direction and then another. Then he started to back and came up on the sidewalk, scaring several women and children.

"Whoa! Get up!" screamed Bob Bangs, more frightened than ever. "Whoa, I say! What in the old Harry is in the beast, anyway!"

"Look out there!" shouted a man in the crowd. "You'll go through a window next."

"Bob, let me lead him into the street," cried Randy, rushing up and catching the horse by the bridle.

"You let my horse alone!" shouted the rich boy, unreasonably. "I can manage him well enough."

"Very well," answered Randy, quietly, and dropped his hold. As he did so the steed made a plunge along the sidewalk for several yards, knocking over a barber's pole and a newsstand.

"Stop dot! Vot you mean py dot?" yelled the German barber, rushing from his establishment in alarm.

"Get along there, you brute!" cried Bob Bangs, savagely, and struck the horse once more. Again the steed swerved, and made a half turn and began to back.

"Stop him!"

"He is going into the window!"

Crash! And then followed a jingle of glass, and into the window of a grocery next to the barber shop backed the horse, until his hind hoofs rested on a row of canned tomatoes and sardines. Bob Bangs gave a yell of fear and terror and dropped to the sidewalk and then caught the horse by the head. The groceryman came forth from his store in a hurry, and a bitter argument ensued, while a big crowd began to collect. In the end Bob Bangs had to promise to pay for all damage done, and led his horse away by hand, too fearful of further trouble to mount once more.

Randy did not wait to see the end of the dispute, for the train was now due and he had just time enough to hurry to the depot and get aboard the cars. He dropped into the first seat that came to hand and laughed heartily.

"You seem to be enjoying yourself," said a man sitting near.

"I just saw something very funny," answered our hero, and told what it was. The man laughed, too.

"It puts me in mind of the time I tried to ride the mule in the circus. It was a trick animal and got me into seven kinds of trouble."

Randy had not had many opportunities to ride on the cars and he enjoyed the trip to Tarrytown very much. Noon found him in the city named and he crossed the river on the ferryboat. Then he hunted up a cheap but neat restaurant, where he got dinner.

"No use of bothering Mr. Shalley just at noon hour," he thought, and so did not go around to the steamboat man's office until one o'clock. A clerk was present who said his employer would come in at two o'clock, so our hero had another hour to wait.

"Is your name Randy Thompson?" questioned the clerk. When told that it was, he continued: "Mr. Shalley is expecting you. I believe you are to be one of the new deckhands."

"Yes."

"I hope you find the work agreeable."

"So do I."

"The other new hand didn't last long."

"How long?"

"Just one week."

"What was the matter?"

"I believe he said he couldn't get along with Polk, the purser."

"I hope I don't have any trouble with anybody," said Randy, anxiously. "I am willing to work hard."

"You'll find Captain Hadley a fine man to deal with. I think he is one of the nicest captains on the river."

"What do you do here?"

"Oh, I am general office clerk. My name is Bart Sandwood."

"I am glad to know you, Mr. Sandwood," answered our hero, and smiled. "I hope business is good with the steamer."

"Travel has been very good and we are getting our share of freight. The other lines bother us some, but not a great deal."

"Is the *Helen Shalley* one of the big boats of the river?"

"Not one of the largest, but she is by no means a small boat. Then you haven't seen her?"

"Not yet, but I hope to soon."

"She will be on her way down the river this afternoon. She runs from New York to Albany one day and back the next. She doesn't run on Sundays."

"I am glad of that. I don't care to work on Sunday."

"Well, you'll have to do a little. When there are no passengers on board, that is the time to put things in order."

"True enough. I am afraid I will be green."

"Were you never a deckhand before?"

"Never."

At this the clerk gave a low whistle.

"I don't know if Captain Hadley will like that or not. He is a very strict man, even though kind."

"I shall do my best to please him."

"Early in the spring we had two green hands, but they couldn't learn at all, and the captain said they were more bother than they were worth."

"I am sure I can learn—anyway, I mean to try."

"You certainly look bright enough to learn. The other fellows were illiterate foreigners and always tumbling over their own feet. One dropped a trunk on a passenger's foot and the other broke open a box with some fine dishes. That capped the climax, and the captain got rid of them just as soon as he could find some other hands to take their places," concluded Bart Sandwood.

CHAPTER XV

RANDY AS A DECKHAND

WHEN Mr. Andrew Shalley came in he was full of business. He nodded pleasantly to Randy.

"I will see you in a little while," he said, and turned to his clerk. Then Bart Sandwood was sent off on an errand and the steamboat owner turned to look over some letters that had come in.

"Now I am at liberty," he said, pleasantly, shaking hands. "Are you ready for work?"

"Yes, sir," answered Randy, promptly.

"Good! Have you ever been on a large river steamer?"

"No, Mr. Shalley, but I am willing to do all I possibly can to make myself truly useful."

"Well, if I am any judge of character, you'll get along. All you've got to do is to keep your eyes open and obey orders. We have one old deckhand, Pat Malloy. He will teach you what to do."

"When can I go to work?"

"The boat will be along down the river soon. I'll take you on board, as I want to see the captain. As soon as you are settled I'll have you fitted out with a uniform."

"How much will that cost me?"

"In your case it won't cost anything."

"You are very kind."

"Remember, I take a personal interest in you, Randy, and I want to see you get along. Do your duty and rest assured I shall not forget you."

"I don't think I'll disappoint you, Mr. Shalley."

Randy waited around the office until it was almost time for the steamboat to make a landing. Then he went down to the dock with his newly-found friend. Here were a number of passengers, and also a quantity of baggage and freight.

Presently the *Helen Shalley* hove into sight, with flags flying bravely in the breeze. As Randy had been told, she was not a particularly large steamboat, but she was well proportioned and graceful, and well liked by those who patronized her. We will get better acquainted with the craft as our story proceeds.

As soon as a landing was made, Mr. Shalley went on board, taking Randy with him. Captain Hadley was at hand.

"So this is the new deckhand, eh?" said the captain, in bluff tones. "Pretty strong, are you?"

"I think so," answered Randy, respectfully.

"Well, you'll have to be, to stand this work. Know anything about handling trunks and such stuff?"

"Not a great deal, but I think I can learn."

"We are shorthanded, so you can jump right in," went on the captain of the steamboat.

"Yes, sir. Who will tell me what to do?"

"Pat Malloy. He is the head man of the gang. Here, Malloy," he called out.

"Aye, aye, sur," answered a brawny and jolly-looking Irishman, coming forward and touching his cap.

"Here's your new hand."

Pat Malloy looked at Randy in some astonishment. Our hero was neatly dressed and did not look as if he was used to hard labor.

"Sure an' it's only a boy," murmured the head deckhand.

"He says he can work. Give him a chance," put in Andrew Shalley.

There was plenty to do, and Randy threw off his coat, took off his collar and tie, and pitched in. The labor was by no means easy, and he had not the trick of throwing up a trunk to the best advantage, yet he did very well, and Pat Malloy nodded approvingly.

"Sure, an' ye do better nor some o' thim foreigners already," he declared. "Kape it up an' we'll git along foine together."

Captain Hadley and Andrew Shalley watched the work for several minutes, and then walked to the cabin of the steamboat. Here the owner of the boat told something about Randy.

"I want you to give him a chance even if he is a bit green," said he. "I want the lad to get along."

"He shall have all the chance possible," answered Captain Hadley. "I am glad to get a hand who is intelligent."

Then the two conversed upon private matters until the boat was ready to leave Nyack.

"Good-by, my boy!" cried Mr. Shalley, on leaving. "Take good care of yourself, and let me know how you get along."

"Thank you, I will," answered our hero.

"It may be hard work at first, but you'll get used to it."

"I am not afraid of hard work."

"The captain will give you a uniform in a few days."

The gangplanks were hauled in, the lines cast off, and with a hoarse whistle the *Helen Shalley* continued on her course down the Hudson. There was a small Italian band on board, consisting of two violins, a harp and a clarionet, and they struck up a popular air.

The work at the dock had somewhat exhausted Randy, who was not used to handling such heavy stuff so quickly, but he took pains to conceal his feelings.

"I am not going to back down, no matter how hard the work is," he told himself. "Others can do it and so can I."

Among the deckhands was a tall, limber American man named Jones. He came up to Randy after the work was done.

"Malloy told me to show you around the boat and give you some pointers," said Jones. "Come ahead."

They passed from one end of the steamboat to the other, through all of the three decks, and Jones named over the various parts and told what the deckhands were expected to do. Then they went below and he told of some work there. Lastly he took Randy to the sleeping quarters.

"This is my bunk," said Jack Jones. "That will be yours over there. When you get the chance, I'll advise you to air your bedding. You can do it after we tie up in New York and the passengers go ashore."

The quarters were small, but not any smaller than Randy's garret apartment in the cottage. Everything was kept as clean as wax, for both Malloy and Jones were enemies to dirt. Randy was glad to learn this and resolved to give the others no cause for complaint regarding his own personal habits.

"Some boats are very dirty and the bunks not fit for a dog to sleep in," said Jack Jones. "But Malloy won't allow it on this boat, and I won't have it either."

"And I am with you," answered our hero.

"Came from a farm, didn't you?"

"Yes, but our family wasn't on the farm long."

"I came from a farm myself."

"How long have you been on this boat?"

"Came the middle of last season."

"Do you like it?"

"If I didn't I shouldn't be here."

"I suppose that is so."

"Captain Hadley is a fine man to work for. He is strict but fair, and that is what I like."

"What about the others?"

"The mate, Tom Blossom, is nice, too. The man we all hate is Peter Polk, the purser."

"What's the matter with him?"

"Well, between you and me, I think he is a sneak."

"In what way?"

"He is always making trouble for somebody. Nobody seems to like him much, although he attends strictly to business."

"I hope I don't have trouble with Mr. Polk."

"Well, you will have to watch yourself."

Several other landings were made, and promptly at the appointed time the *Helen Shalley* swung into her dock at New York City and the remaining passengers went ashore. Then began the labor of unloading the baggage and freight, after which the deck was swabbed up, the brass-work polished, and such baggage as was at hand taken on board for transportation up the river the next day.

When he had finished his day's labors Randy was tired and perfectly willing to rest for a while. He had had a good supper and might have gone directly to bed, but instead he sat up to write a letter to the folks at home, telling his father and mother of his day's experience.

Our hero had to go ashore to post the communication, and once out in the street he resolved to take a little walk around before returning to the steamboat. He was soon walking along West Street, and then took to a side street running up to the avenues.

Now, although our hero did not know it, he had chosen one of the worst streets in this part of the great city. It was filled with tenements and groggeries of the lowest description, and the sidewalks swarmed with all sorts of low characters.

He had scarcely walked two squares before a rough-looking fellow jostled him. The next instant Randy felt a hand in his pocket.

"Stop that!" cried Randy. But the fellow was already running up the street. Our hero clapped his hand in the pocket and discovered that eighty cents in change was missing.

"I am not going to lose that money!" he told himself, with vigor. "I may be a greeny, but I'll give that thief some trouble."

At first he thought to cry out, but then reconsidered the matter and remained silent. He set off after the thief, and away went man and boy along the crowded thoroughfare.

The man evidently thought he could lose himself in the crowd, but by the aid of the street lights, Randy kept him in sight. He passed along for two blocks and then turned into a side street and then into a blind alley.

Our hero managed to keep him in view and saw him spring up the steps of a dilapidated tenement house. The man ran through the lower hallway and into the back yard, piled high with rubbish of all kinds. Here he hid behind some empty boxes.

Randy was soon in the yard and gazing around eagerly. As he did so he saw a thin and pale girl of about ten standing near. Soon she came up to him timidly.

"Did you see a man run in here?" said Randy.

"Yes," she answered, but in a hesitating voice.

"Where did he go?"

"I don't dare tell you," whispered the girl.

"Why not?"

"That is Bill Hosker."

"And who is Bill Hosker?"

"Don't you know him?" And the little girl's eyes opened in astonishment.

"No, I don't."

"Bill Hosker is the boss around here. He does just as he pleases. If anybody crosses him Bill 'most kills them."

"Oh, he's a bully, is that it?"

"Yes."

"Well, where did he go?"

"You won't tell him I told you?"

"No."

"He crawled in behind those boxes," answered the little girl and then ran away.

Randy waited to hear no more, but made a dash for the boxes. As he did so, the fellow who had robbed him leaped up, club in hand.

"Go out of here!" he cried, in a hoarse voice. "I don't want anything to do with a kid like you."

"You give me my money," answered Randy, vigorously. "I am not going to let the like of you rob me."

"Ho! ho! Hear the kid talk! Go away, before I maul ye!" And Bill Hosker brandished his club.

But our hero was not to be daunted thus readily, and looking around he espied a stick and picked it up. Then he advanced upon Bill Hosker, who promptly leaped to the top of a big packing case. The next instant he came down upon Randy, bearing him to the ground. Our hero tried to defend himself, but it was useless. He was crushed beneath that heavy weight, and then the rascal gave him a crack on the head that stretched him senseless.

CHAPTER XVI

IN NEW YORK CITY

"WILL he live, mamma?"

"I think so, Rose. But he has been badly misused."

"Bill Hosker ought to be locked up for it."

"Nobody will lock Bill up. He has too much influence with the politicians," answered the woman.

She was bending over Randy, who was still unconscious. Mother and daughter had carried our hero from the yard to their room in the rear of the tenement. Nobody else had been around. The girl had witnessed Bill Hosker's nefarious deed and had at once summoned her parent.

Mrs. Clare was a poor widow lady who supported herself by sewing. Rose was her only child and did what she could to help her mother. Sewing did not pay well, and the Clares had all they could do to make both ends meet.

But Mrs. Clare had a warm heart and so had

Rose, and it pained them greatly to see Randy so mistreated. They carried him into their one room and placed him on their bed and did what they could for him.

At last he opened his eyes and stared around him. Then he sat up slowly.

"Where am I?" he asked, faintly.

"We brought you into the house—mother and I," answered Rose. "Don't you remember, Bill Hosker struck you down?"

"Oh, yes; I remember that now." Randy took a deep breath and put his hand to his head. "He hit me pretty hard, didn't he?"

"I am afraid he did," answered Mrs. Clare. "It was a shame, too."

"Where is he now?"

"He ran away."

"He stole eighty cents from me."

"Perhaps he took more," said Rose. "He went through your pockets after he knocked you down. I saw him do it."

With his head still aching, our hero felt in first one pocket and then another. He gave something like a groan.

"Every cent is gone!"

"How much did you have?"

"Between four and five dollars."

"I am sorry for you," said Mrs. Clare. "But I am afraid you will never see your money again."

"Does that rascal live around here?"

"Sometimes. He comes and goes to suit himself. I suppose he will stay away now for a while."

"Is there any use of my reporting this to the police, do you think?"

"I don't think so. He once took my pocket-book from the table here—I am sure of it—but when I reported it to the police nothing was done. They said his word was as good as mine."

"How long have I been here?"

"About half an hour."

"Then he has had a good chance to get away. Did you bring me here?"

"Yes."

"You are very kind, Mrs.——"

"I am Mrs. Clare and this is my daughter Rose."

"And I am Randy Thompson, a deckhand on the Hudson River steamboat *Helen Shalley*."

"Oh!" Mrs. Clare paused for a moment. "Do you know Mr. Polk, the purser?"

"Yes, but not very well. I just got the job as a deckhand to-day."

"Mr. Polk is a relative of mine by marriage."

"I see."

"We—that is—well, we are not very good friends," went on Mrs. Clare.

"Mamma thinks Mr. Polk hasn't been honest with us," put in Rose, quickly. "I don't think so either."

"Rose, you must not talk so!"

"But it is true, isn't it?" returned the daughter.

"I may be misjudging Cousin Peter," said Mrs. Clare. "You see," she added, by way of an explanation, "my cousin Peter Polk had the settlement of my husband's affairs when he died, and I have always imagined that—well, that Rose and I did not get exactly what was coming to us."

"Mamma thought the account was three hundred dollars short," said Rose, who was inclined to be blunt.

"Couldn't you get a clear statement?" questioned Randy, with interest.

"We got a statement, but it was not clear to me," answered Mrs. Clare.

As soon as he felt able to do so, Randy got on his feet. He felt rather dizzy and he had a large lump over his left ear, where he had been struck by the club.

"See here," he said, when he was ready to depart, "I am much obliged to you for what you have done. But I'd like you to do more, if you will. As soon as this Bill Hosker comes back to this neighborhood let me know. You'll always find me on board of the *Helen Shalley*."

"I'll let you know," answered Rose. "But don't let Bill Hosker know who told you, or he'll want to kill me."

When Randy got back to the steamboat he felt so weak he could scarcely walk on board. Jones came forward to meet him.

"Say, you ain't been drinking, have you?" he demanded, as he saw our hero stagger.

"No, I don't drink," answered Randy. "I've been knocked down and robbed."

And sitting down on a bench he told his story to the other deckhand, and let Jones feel of the lump on his head.

"I was going to warn you when you went ashore, but I thought you'd be wise enough to keep out of trouble. It's a shame."

"They told me it wouldn't do any good to tell the police."

"I am afraid not. Such things happen pretty often in that kind of a neighborhood."

Randy was glad enough to turn in. He bathed

the lump with cold water and put on some witch-hazel, which made it feel better. Despite the adventure he slept soundly until it was time to turn out in the morning.

"I suppose you'll want some money," said Jones. "I can lend you a dollar till pay day, if you wish."

"Thank you," returned Randy. "You are kind, and I'll accept the loan. I'll pay you back just as soon as I get my pay. I hate to be without a cent in my pocket."

"I have been there myself and know just how it feels," answered Jones. He had, in his rough way, taken a fancy to our hero, which feeling was reciprocated.

There was plenty to do before the steamboat left the dock at New York City, and Randy's arms ached when the command came to cast off the lines. He had done his full share of the labor, and Pat Malloy nodded approvingly.

"Kape it up an' you'll be all roight," said the head deckhand.

The trip to Albany that day had much of novelty in it for Randy. There was a good deal of work, of which he had not dreamed before, yet there were also times when he could look at the scenery as the big craft glided along. At the newsstand on board there was a big folding map of the river, showing the different towns and points of interest, and this the standkeeper loaned him for a couple of hours. He studied the map closely and was soon able to recognize certain points as they appeared.

Several days slipped by and Randy felt quite at home on board. He had been supplied with the regulation deckhand's outfit; dark blue shirt and trousers, and a cap to match, and looked very well when thus attired. He was getting acquainted with the work and could handle a trunk, or a box or barrel almost as well as Jones or Malloy.

"How does the boy do?" asked Captain Hadley of Malloy.

"It's the new broom as swapes clane," answered the head deckhand. "I ain't braggin' yit, captain."

"But he is doing all right so far?"

"Aye, aye, sur—very well indade."

"I am glad to hear it. Mr. Shalley told me the boy needed the job. His father is on the sick list, and he has got to do what he can to help support his parents."

"I reckon he'll be all right," answered Pat Malloy. "He's better than thim foreigners, anyway." To him, the only foreigners were Italians and Germans. He did not think himself one, although he had come from the "ould sod" less than six years before.

CHAPTER XVII

THE PURSER HAS HIS SAY

One night, when the steamboat was tied up at Albany, Randy donned his street clothes and hunted up the place where Jack Bartlett lived. He found his former friend at home and glad to see him.

"Come in," said Jack, shaking hands. "How have you been since we met last?"

"Pretty fair, Jack. And how have you been?"

"I'm all right. I've got a job. That is why I haven't used my boat pass."

"A job?"

"Yes, I am working in the same place where father has a position."

"Then you are not going to school again?"

"Not for the present." Jack lowered his voice. "You see, father isn't earning any too much, so I—well, I thought I'd help the family along."

The two friends sat down in the parlor and our

hero told his tale, and then Jack related some of his own experiences.

"My father is in hopes that he can get at Mr. Bangs before long," said Jack. "The trouble is, some papers are missing. He had them in a desk at the works, but when he came away he couldn't find them."

"Perhaps Mr. Bangs got them."

"It is possible, but father can't prove it."

"Have you seen or heard anything of Bob Bangs lately?"

"He is along the Hudson somewhere—on a vacation with his mother."

"I met him when he was getting a horse," answered our hero and told of what had happened.

"I wish I had been there!" cried Jack, laughing heartily. "I'll wager Bob was as mad as seventeen hornets."

"Yes, indeed. He must have had a good bill to pay for damages."

Randy spent a pleasant two hours with Jack and then went back to the boat, Jack promising to visit the craft some night when the *Helen Shalley* should tie up at Albany again.

So far matters had gone well on board. Randy was much amused by the passengers, especially those who were peculiar in their manners. There was one fussy old gentleman who went up and down the river twice a week. He always wanted to sit in a corner in the shade and asked a dozen times a day if they weren't behindhand.

"We are exactly on time," said Randy, to him, one day.

"Hum!" cried the old gentleman, consulting a watch he carried. "I think we are twenty minutes behindhand."

"We haven't been twenty minutes behindhand since I've been on the boat," said Randy, as he moved off.

The old gentleman grumbled to himself and restored his timepiece to his pocket.

A minute later Randy saw an Englishman saunter along the deck and stop close to the old gentleman. Randy had noticed the Englishman before, because he spoke with a strong Cockney accent—that is, he dropped h's where they were wanted and put them in when not needed. At this time the steamboat was just approaching the Highlands.

The Englishman pointed to the Highlands with his cane and addressed the old gentleman.

"Hexcuse me," he said, "but are those the 'Ighlands you brag about in this country?"

"The islands?" was the astonished reply.

"Why, no, sir, those are not islands at all. Have you never studied geography? An island is entirely surrounded by water," continued the fussy old gentleman.

"Oh, you mean hilands. I don't mean them at all, don't you know. I repeat, are those the 'Ighlands you talk about so much?" went on the Cockney, blandly.

"They are not islands, sir—they are the Highlands," shouted the old gentleman.

"Just exactly what I said, sir—the 'Ighlands."

"No, not islands—Highlands."

"Hexactly."

"But you said islands."

"No, I did not say hilands, I said the 'Ighlands," went on the Cockney. "Hevidently you don't understand good, plain Henglish," and he walked off in disgust.

"The imp, the blithering imp," growled the old gentleman. "May he never come near me again!"

At one of the landings a barrel for use on the boat broke, spilling some fancy flour on the deck. Randy was clearing up the muss when the purser, Peter Polk, came along. Our hero did not witness his approach, and consequently the purser received some dust on his shoes, which had just been polished.

"Hi! hi! Have a care there!" he cried. "What do you mean by covering me with dust?"

"Excuse me, sir," said Randy, hastily. "I didn't see you coming."

"I just had those shoes shined!"

"I am sorry, sir."

"You're the new man, eh?"

"Yes, sir."

"You're a blockhead, it seems to me," went on the purser, who was in particularly bad humor that day.

An angry remark rose to Randy's lips, but he repressed it.

"You be more careful in the future, or you'll get into trouble," grumbled the purser, and walked away.

The moment the purser was gone Jones came up to our hero.

"Brute, ain't he?" he said, in a low voice.

"He called me a blockhead." Randy's eyes were flashing.

"Don't you mind him, lad. He is sour all the way through—he don't seem to be able to help it."

"I didn't see him coming."

"He should have looked where he was walking."

"I don't wonder the hands don't like him," went on Randy. "I don't think Captain Hadley would have spoken so."

"Not a bit of it—the captain's a gentleman, every inch of him."

"How do he and the purser get along together?"

"None too good, so I've been told. I wish we had a man in place of Polk."

"So do I."

"More than likely, when he comes to pay you your wages, he'll take out the price of a shoe shine."

"Would he really be mean enough to do that?"

"Polk is about mean enough to do anything."

There the talk ended and Randy finished up his work. The day passed, and when the steamboat tied up that night Randy was more than usually sleepy. It was very warm, and he went on the upper deck to get a breath of fresh air.

"See here," said the purser, coming up to him rather suddenly. "Are you talking about me?"

"Talking about you?" repeated our hero, somewhat puzzled.

"That is what I said."

"Not particularly, Mr. Polk."

"Somebody on this boat is telling tales about me, and I don't like it."

To this Randy made no answer.

"Have you heard any stories?" went on Peter Polk.

"What kind of stories?"

"That I was going to leave the steamboat?"

"No, sir."

"No stories at all?"

"No, sir."

"Humph!" And with this the purser walked away.

"What did he want now?" asked Jones, coming up a little later.

"Wanted to know if I had been circulating stories about him."

"Did you tell him no?"

"I did."

"I've heard a story—in a roundabout way—that Mr. Shalley is getting tired of the way Polk runs the money matters on this boat."

"Does he run all the money matters?"

"Sure—that is a purser's business. He does the buying—or most of it—too."

"I see."

"I don't believe he buys to advantage," went on Jones, closing one eye suggestively.

"I don't understand."

"Maybe he buys at two prices—some of 'em do, you know."

Randy did not know, but he did not say so.

"I knew a purser once—on the *Sea Shell*—who used to pay one price for a thing and then charge the owners of the vessel another price. At last they caught him at it and sent him to prison."

This opened Randy's eyes to what his fellow-deckhand was driving at.

"Do you imagine Polk is that sort?"

"He is certainly close."

"So you said before. Well, he ought to be watched."

"Oh, it's not my affair," said Jones. "Say, I am going to bed," he added.

"So am I," said Randy, and retired, thinking of what Jones had said and also of what the Clares had told him regarding Peter Polk.

CHAPTER XVIII

A MEETING ON THE RIVER

Two weeks passed and Randy felt quite at home on board of the steamboat. He had learned his duties fully and was giving satisfaction to Captain Hadley and Pat Malloy.

His only enemy seemed to be Polk the purser, who was as disagreeable as possible. Our hero did his best to steer clear of the fellow, and in a measure succeeded.

One evening, while the boat was tied up at the dock in New York Randy chanced to look ashore when he saw Rose Clare motioning to him. He at once joined the girl.

"I came down to tell you that Bill Hosker was around yesterday," said the girl to our hero.

"Is he around now?" questioned Randy, quickly.

"No, he went away yesterday evening. He was only around about two hours."

"I wish I had seen him."

"I thought you'd like to know about it. I came down last night, but a man here told me you were at Albany."

"Yes, we come to New York every other night, not counting Sundays."

"I think Bill Hosker will come again soon. I suppose he thinks you have given up trying to find him."

"Well, I haven't given it up, Rose. How are things going with yourself and your mother?"

"Not very good."

"Can't she get much sewing to do?"

"She and I made only five dollars and a quarter last week."

"And what rent do you pay?"

"Six dollars a month for just the one room."

"That is certainly hard. I wish I could help you, but I can't—at least, not now."

"We wouldn't want help, if only we could get more sewing."

"I'll ask Captain Hadley about it. He has a wife and a family of girls."

Randy was as good as his word. He met the captain the next day, when the officer appeared to have little to do.

"Captain, may I speak to you a moment?" he

asked, respectfully, and at the same time tipping his cap.

"What is it, Randy?"

"I know a poor lady in New York who does sewing for a living. She is anxious to get more work and I am anxious to help her, if I possibly can. Do you know of anybody who would like some sewing done—your wife or anybody else?"

"Hm! I don't know," answered the steamboat captain. "I'll remember what you say and see. Is that all?"

"Yes, sir."

"Where does the poor woman live?"

"Not far from our landing place in New York." He gave the street and number. "It isn't a nice neighborhood, but it is the best the woman can afford," he added.

"Yes, I know many folks in New York who live in bad neighborhoods simply because they cannot afford something better. I will speak to my wife about this."

The captain did as he had promised. Mrs. Hadley was going to New York the next day and said she would call upon Mrs. Clare. The family lived in Albany, so that the captain was home every other night.

Mrs. Hadley was as good as her word. She

was a Christian woman, a worker in the church, and she became at once interested in Mrs. Clare and her daughter Rose.

"This is no place for Rose," said she. "This foul air is bad for her."

"I know it—but I do not see how I can turn myself," said Mrs. Clare, with a sigh. Poverty had completely broken her spirit.

The captain's wife looked over some of the sewing that Mrs. Clare had done and soon learned that the woman was a clever seamstress. Then she made an offer.

"If you wish, you can come to my home with me," she said. "You can sew for me, and Rose can go to school and also help around the house. I will give you five dollars a week and your board."

"I will accept gladly!" cried the poor woman, and burst into tears of gratitude.

It was arranged that Mrs. Clare should leave New York on the following Saturday. She was to sell off the most of her things—alas! there were not many articles to dispose of! and the others were to be transferred to Albany on the boat.

"My cousin, Mr. Polk, will be surprised to learn of this move," said Mrs. Clare to the captain's wife.

"What, is he your cousin?" queried Mrs. Hadley.

"Yes, by marriage," and then Mrs. Clare told her tale of suffering, to which the captain's wife gave a willing ear.

"I must speak of this to my husband," said Mrs. Hadley. "I do not think he likes Mr. Polk very much."

On Saturday Randy was moving some baggage from one side of the lower deck to the other when Peter Polk came along. As luck would have it, some trunks were in the way, so that the purser could not pass.

"Look here, you blockhead, why don't you keep this gangway clear?" he roared to Randy.

"I am trying to clear it now," answered our hero, as calmly as he could.

"It ought to be kept clear always. Who ordered this stuff here, anyway?"

"Mr. Malloy."

"He had no business to do it."

"Why didn't I, I'd like to be after knowin'?" came in a voice from behind the purser, and the head deckhand appeared on the scene.

"Oh, so you're here, are you?" sneered Peter Polk.

"I am that, Mr. Polk. I ordered thim trunks

there. Have ye anything against it?" demanded Malloy, boldly. "If ye have, report to the captain."

"You're blocking the whole gangway."

"Thim trunks had to be shifted, an' Thompson is shiftin' 'em."

"Humph!"

"I know me juty on this boat, Mr. Polk."

"Well—er—hurry up then and clear this gangway," grumbled the purser, and walked away. Malloy closed one eye and looked at Randy suggestively with the other.

"He knew he had no right to interfere—it's not his line o' juty," said the head deckhand.

Randy completed his work and then went to one of the upper decks, to fix some of the awnings. To his surprise he found Mrs. Clare and Rose there, in conversation with Peter Polk.

"Going to Albany?" the purser was saying. "What for?"

"I have a situation there, and Rose is going also," answered the poor woman.

"What kind of a situation?"

"I am to sew for Mrs. Hadley."

"Not the captain's wife?"

"Yes."

At this announcement the face of the purser

dropped. Evidently the news did not please him.

"You won't find that very pleasant," he said.

"It will be better than starving in the city, Peter."

"How much is she going to pay you?"

Mrs. Clare told him.

"That is not a fortune. You ought to be able to earn more in New York."

"I couldn't get the work."

"I might have gotten something for you, if you had let me know," went on Peter Polk.

"Thank you—I prefer to look out for myself," answered Mrs. Clare, coolly.

"This looks as if I was letting one of my relatives live on charity," pursued the purser.

"I do not consider it a charity."

"How did the captain's wife hear of you?"

"Why, she—there is a boy on this boat—there he is—he spoke to the captain about it."

"You mean Randy Thompson?"

"Yes, that is his name."

"He got the place for you?"

"Yes."

"How did you happen to know him?"

"It's a long story. He was knocked down and robbed and Rose and I went to his assistance.

But we must go now. Mrs. Hadley wanted us to do some sewing for the captain while on this trip," and Mrs. Clare walked away, followed by Rose. Peter Polk gazed after them thoughtfully.

"I hope she doesn't get the captain's wife too much interested in her affairs," he muttered to himself. "I shouldn't care to have the old accounts raked up in court."

CHAPTER XIX

AN UNLOOKED-FOR ENCOUNTER

It was now early in September and the travel down the river was particularly heavy, for many folks who had been away for a vacation were returning to the metropolis. Baggage kept pouring in until the lower deck was practically filled.

"This is a banner season, so Malloy tells me," said Jones to Randy.

"I know there is lots of work," answered our hero, whose arms ached not a little.

"Never mind, I've got good news."

"What is that?"

"Mr. Shalley is going to allow us an extra five dollars this month."

"Good enough."

Randy had received several letters from home. Matters were going smoothly and Mr. Thompson was feeling better every day. The garden was doing finely. In one letter Mrs. Thompson wrote that there had been two strikes at the iron works, each due to Mr. Bangs' overbearing manner towards his workmen.

"I thought he'd have trouble sooner or later," said Randy to himself, as he perused the communication. "What a pity that Mr. Bartlett isn't in charge."

One fine afternoon the *Helen Shalley* was steaming down the river as usual and Randy was near the bow, coiling up a hawser, when he noticed a sloop some distance ahead. It was tacking in an uncertain manner, as if the party on board did not know much about sailing such a craft.

The sloop was directly in the path of the big steamboat, and the latter gave a warning whistle and then turned to one side. As she did this the sloop turned in the same direction.

"Hullo! What does that fellow in the sloop mean?" cried Randy to Jones, who was near.

"What's the matter?"

"He'll be run down if he doesn't look out."

"Some fool that doesn't know how to sail a boat, I guess," said the other deckhand.

Swiftly the steamboat and the sloop drew close to one another. The big boat let out another warning blast, and again the pilot turned her out of her course. But the sloop also turned.

THE SHOCK THREW BOB BANGS OVERBOARD.—P. 172.

Randy of the River

"There is only one young fellow on board," said Jones. "Look, he acts as if he was scared out of his wits."

"I know him!" fairly shouted our hero.

"You do?"

"Yes, it is Bob Bangs, the rich young fellow I told you about."

"The fellow who couldn't manage his hoss?"

"The same."

"Well, he doesn't seem to know no more about his boat than he did about that hoss," was the deckhand's comment.

"We are going to run into him!" gasped Randy.

"No, he is going to run into us."

"It will amount to the same thing—so far as he is concerned."

"Maybe—but it will be his fault if he gets drowned."

Another warning whistle now rang out, but was of no avail. The sloop swerved again and then came squarely up to the big steamboat, which was now backing water furiously.

"Stop! Don't run me down!" screamed Bob Bangs. He was fairly white with terror.

His cries were cut short by the crash as the sloop struck. The bow was splintered, and the shock threw Bob Bangs overboard. Luckily he was far enough away to escape the paddle-wheel, as the *Helen Shalley* continued to go ahead despite the fact that her engines had been reversed.

The first surprise over, Randy was quick to act. Not far away was a life preserver having a line attached to it and this he took from its hooks. He waited for the rich boy to appear. Soon he came up, spluttering.

"Catch the preserver!" called out our hero and cast the article in such a skillful manner that it fell within easy reach.

"Save me! Save me!" gasped the rich youth, throwing his arms wildly about him.

"Take hold of the life preserver!" called out half a hundred people at once. Then several other cries rang out.

At last the motion of the water washed the life preserver up against Bob Bangs' arm. He clutched at it desperately. By this time the steamboat had come to a standstill, and it was an easy matter for Randy and Jones to pull the rich youth towards the vessel. Then a rope ladder was lowered and Bob Bangs came up to the deck, dripping with water.

"Well, young man, you had a narrow escape,"

said Captain Hadley, as he pushed his way through the crowd to the spot.

"I know it, and it's all your fault!" whined Bob Bangs.

"My fault? Nonsense!"

"You ran me down! I'll have the law on you for it."

"Don't talk like a fool, young man. I was in the wheelhouse myself with the pilot and saw just how you acted. Evidently you don't know much about handling boats."

"I know all about them," insisted the rich youth. But this was a falsehood, as Randy well knew. Bob could row and that was about all.

"You'll have to pay for smashing my boat," went on the rich boy, after a pause. "And you'll have to pay for wetting my new suit," he added, gazing ruefully at the natty outing suit he had donned but an hour before.

"You'll not get a cent out of me," said Captain Hadley, firmly. "This accident was clearly of your own making. We gave you plenty of room, but you turned directly into our course twice. Be thankful that you weren't ground up under the paddle-wheel."

"Yes, and be thankful that Randy Thompson threw you a life preserver," put in Jones.

At the mention of our hero's name Bob Bangs looked around in surprise. He had not noticed Randy before.

"What, you here!" he exclaimed and did not seem particularly happy over the meeting.

"I am," answered Randy.

"Did you throw out that line with the preserver?" asked the captain.

"I did, sir," and Randy touched his cap.

"I am glad to know it," and the captain's face showed his appreciation of Randy's prompt action.

"What are you doing here—in that outfit?" asked Bob Bangs, curiously.

"I am a deckhand on this steamboat."

"Pooh! a deckhand!" and the rich boy's nose went up into the air in disdain. He would give Randy no credit for helping to save his life.

"Clear the deck, please!" called out Captain Hadley, to the crowd that was pressing in on all sides. "The excitement is over. The boy is safe."

"I want you to put me ashore," said Bob Bangs.

"We'll make a landing a mile below here," said the Captai

"I don't want to go to the next landing."

"Sorry, but we can't turn back," answered Captain Hadley.

"What about my boat?"

"We'll take it in tow."

This was done, and in a few minutes the *Helen Shalley* had resumed her journey. Bob Bangs was led to one of the staterooms and offered a dry suit of clothes, which he put on.

"I'll take your name and address," said Captain Hadley.

"What for?"

"As a matter of record. And remember, I want the clothing returned."

"Humph! Maybe my father will sue you for damages!"

"If he does he will lose the case."

Inside of five minutes the next landing place was made, and Bob Bangs went ashore, taking his wet suit with him. The damaged sloop was tied up at the dock, and having discharged and taken on passengers and baggage the steamboat sped on her way once more.

"He's as mad as a wet hen," said Jones to Randy. "And he ought to be thankful for having his life spared."

"He always was a mean sort of fellow," answered our hero. "And his folks are just as mean as he is."

"Then maybe they will try to make trouble for the steamboat owner."

Amos Bangs did try to make trouble. Two days after the accident on the river Andrew Shalley received a letter which ran in part as follows:

"As you perhaps know, my son, Robert Bangs, was out on the Hudson on the 6th inst., in his sloop, when, without any cause whatsoever, your steamboat, the *Helen Shalley,* ran into his boat, smashed it completely and put him in peril of his life.

"I am a man of few words, sir, and I demand damages for this outrage. If you wish to settle, you may send me your check for one thousand dollars; if not, I will sue you for that amount."

CHAPTER XX

WHAT CAME OF A DEMAND

THE letter from Amos Bangs worried Andrew Shalley a little and he at once called on Captain Hadley, as soon as the steamboat made a landing at Nyack.

"It seems you ran down a boy a few days ago," said the steamboat owner.

"He tried to run us down," answered the captain, quietly.

"Was he hurt?"

"Not in the least."

"His father wants a thousand dollars' damages."

"I wouldn't pay him a cent."

"Did you run him down?"

"No, he tried to run us down."

"This is no joke, Captain Hadley."

"I know it, Mr. Shalley. But to threaten us with a suit at law is absurd. I can bring a dozen witnesses to prove that the accident was entirely of the boy's making."

"I am glad to hear that," and Andrew Shalley breathed a sigh of relief. He did not care so much for the money, but he wanted to know that Captain Hadley was not to blame.

"That boy acted like a little fool from beginning to end," went on the captain of the steamboat and then told his story. Later Randy was called up, to relate what he had done, and also Jones.

"If there is any trouble some of the passengers will testify for us," said Captain Hadley, and mentioned half a dozen who had said they would stick to the captain, in case of trouble. The passengers were well-known citizens, whose testimony would be sure to carry weight in any court of law.

Having satisfied himself that Amos Bangs had no case against him, the steamboat owner wrote to the rich manufacturer to that effect. By return mail he received this reply:

"Your bluff will not work with me. You are to blame and must pay. If I do not receive your check for one thousand dollars by the middle of next week I shall bring suit. My son is now in bed and under the doctor's care because of the accident."

"Humph! Under the doctor's care, eh?" mused the steamboat owner. "This certainly seems to be serious after all. He will certainly make trouble for me even if he doesn't win his case."

Again the steamboat owner interviewed Captain Hadley, and then the pair called in Randy, to learn what he could tell about the Bangs family in general. Our hero told all he knew, including the trouble Mr. Bartlett was having with the iron manufacturer.

"Evidently he is a man to get money in any manner possible," mused Andrew Shalley. "He will certainly bring suit."

"I don't believe Bob is sick," said Randy. "He must be shamming."

"I wish I knew for sure."

"Perhaps I can find out for you—if you'll give me a day or two off," said our hero, struck by a sudden idea.

"A good plan!" cried Captain Hadley. "Let the lad see what he can do, by all means."

The matter was talked over, and the upshot was that on the next trip of the steamboat Randy went ashore at Catskill, near which town Bob Bangs and his mother were spending their vacation.

From some men at the dock our hero was enabled to find out all about the damaged sloop, which had been returned to Catskill. It was to cost twenty dollars to put the craft in good condition again.

"Those folks are stopping at a small hotel on the Burnham road," said one of the dock men. "It's called the Sharon House."

"Thank you," returned our hero.

He was soon on the way to the Sharon House —since demolished by fire. It did not take him long to cover the distance. As he approached he looked around for some signs of the Bangs family and presently espied Mrs. Bangs lounging in a hammock on a side veranda, reading a novel.

"I wonder if it is possible that Bob is really in bed sick?" he mused. "If he is it's a wonder Mrs. Bangs isn't with him. But then I guess she is a selfish woman, anyway."

Randy walked around the hotel and down to the stable. Here he met a colored boy who helped around the horses.

"Say, can you tell me where I can find Bob Bangs?" he asked, boldly.

"Bob Bangs jest went down to the ball grounds," was the answer, which surprised Randy not a little.

"Where are the grounds?"

"That way," and the colored boy pointed with his hand.

"I thought maybe Bob was sick."

"He ain't sick—he's only pertendin'," answered the colored boy.

Randy said no more but hurried off in the direction of the baseball grounds. Just as he came in sight of the place, he saw a figure ahead that looked familiar to him.

"Unless I am mistaken, that is Bob," he told himself, and hurried closer.

It was indeed Bob Bangs, walking along as if nothing had ever happened to him. He was smoking a cigarette. He passed into the grounds and Randy did the same, and took a seat on a bench directly behind the rich youth.

It was easy to see that Bob Bangs was not suffering physically. He smoked half a dozen cigarettes, and applauded as loudly as anybody when a good play was made.

"Fine game," said a man sitting next to Randy.

"It is," said our hero. He looked at the man

and saw that he was evidently a merchant. "Excuse me, are you from Catskill?"

"I am."

"Do you want to do me a favor if I pay you for it?"

"Well, it won't be a favor if you pay me."

"I may want your assistance and I may not. Do you see that boy there?"

"Yes."

"He doesn't look as if he was sick abed, does he?"

"Sick abed? What sort of a game is this?" and the merchant looked Randy over with much curiosity.

"That boy's father says he is sick in bed. I want to prove that it isn't so."

"What is the game, anyway?"

"He had an accident on the river and he wants damages from a man I work for. It is a put-up job."

"Oh! I've heard of such things before. I know a rascal who cut his foot with an ax and then went down to the railroad and laid the blame on a train. He got five hundred dollars, but, later on, was found out and sent to prison for the deception."

"Well, this isn't exactly like that. Didn't you

hear about a sloop running into the *Helen Shalley* a few days ago?"

"Oh, yes, a friend of mine, a passenger on the boat, told me about it. He said the boy didn't know how to handle the craft."

"Well, that is the boy."

"Indeed!"

"Does he act as if he was hurt or suffering?"

"Not in the least."

"Would you be willing to testify to that fact, if it came to law?"

"Certainly."

"Will you give me your name and address?"

"Here is my card," and the merchant handed it over. He did not add that he occasionally sold Captain Hadley some goods and was glad to do the master of the steamboat a service.

The game was almost at an end when the ball was sent among the spectators. Seeing it coming towards him, Bob Bangs leaped up and tried to catch the sphere. It hit the tips of his fingers, stinging them greatly. Then the ball came towards Randy and he caught it and threw it back into the field.

"What are you doing here?" demanded Bob Bangs, as he caught sight of our hero.

"Watching the game," answered Randy, quietly.

"Humph!"

"Pretty nice game, Bob."

"Humph!" muttered the rich boy again.

"I see you are feeling fine again."

"I am not—I am real sick," answered the rich boy, quickly.

"Sick in bed, eh?" went on our hero, with a grin.

"I was in bed."

"Last night, I suppose. So was I."

"I'm sick yet."

"You showed it—by the way you were cheering and yelling."

"When did you come in?"

"Right after you."

"Humph! Have you been watching me?"

"Yes."

"You might be in a better business," sneered the rich boy.

"I don't think so. You need watching. You and your father want to cheat the steamboat company by pretending that you were hurt in that collision, and here you are as well and hearty as ever," added Randy in a loud voice, so that those nearby might hear.

"I ain't well—I'm sick."

"You said that before—but nobody will believe it."

"You're well enough to go to a ball game and yell and smoke cigarettes, anyway," put in the merchant sitting next to Randy.

A good play brought forth a cheer from the crowd which drowned out further talk. In the midst of the temporary excitement Bob Bangs sneaked from the stand and from the ball grounds.

"He feels sick over this," laughed the merchant.

"Well, he can't sue the steamboat company for that sickness," laughed our hero in return.

CHAPTER XXI

RANDY VISITS HIS HOME

As soon as he returned to the steamboat, Randy acquainted Captain Hadley with all he had seen and heard and gave the captain the card of the merchant.

"You have done well, Randy," said the master of the steamboat. "I fancy this will cook Mr. Amos Bangs's goose."

At Nyack, Mr. Shalley came on board and heard what our hero had to say.

"I am glad you have a witness," said he. "I have heard of Mr. Budmister before."

"A good business man," said Captain Hadley. "He will make a good witness—if the case comes to a trial."

But it never did come to a trial. Andrew Shalley received one letter from a lawyer, threatening the suit, and in return wrote back the particulars of what Randy had learned, and added that if he heard any more of the matter he would bring suit against Amos Bangs for conspiracy to defraud. There the matter ended.

The captain was so pleased that when Randy asked for a three-days' leave of absence, that he might visit his home, it was readily granted. The boy was also given some extra pay for his work at Catskill.

Randy's homecoming brought a warm smile to the faces of his father and his mother. His mother kissed him tenderly and his father shook hands.

"How are you feeling, father?"

"I am almost well, Randy. I expect to go to work next week."

"But not in a cellar," said the son, quickly.

"No, Mr. Jackson is going to build a wing on his house and has given me the whole contract."

"That is good."

"I will be able to make more money than if I was working for a boss," went on Mr. Thompson.

"Well, you won't be sorry for that," said Randy, with a smile.

He found matters on the farm moving along nicely. The late vegetables were coming in well and their neighbor, Jerry Borden, had given them a helping hand.

"Say, you're a-gittin' to be a regular sailor, ain't you?" said Sammy to Randy.

"Hardly a sailor," answered Randy, with a laugh. "I am a steamboat deckhand."

"It's about the same thing. Wish I was a sailor."

"Maybe if you sailed on the ocean you'd get seasick, Sammy."

"I wouldn't, nuther. I was readin' about Robinson Crusoe onct. I wish I was cast away on a barren island. It would be lots of fun."

"Especially if you had nothing to eat and to drink."

"Oh, I'd get something from the ship, as Crusoe did."

"If the ship didn't go down in the middle of the ocean."

"When I was on the island I'd sleep every morning as long as I wanted to."

"What would you do if the savages came after you?"

"I'd fight and kill them all—that is, all but one. I'd want that one for my man Friday."

"He ain't going to be no sailor," broke in Mrs. Borden, who overheard the conversation. "He is going out to hunt eggs an' he is a-goin' to do it right now, or I'll get the whip."

"I'll get the eggs," answered Sammy, and hurried off without further delay.

"That boy is crazy to go somewhere all the time," said Mrs. Borden. "He doesn't seem to like the farm a bit."

"Better let him look for work somewhere," said Randy. "Maybe it will cure him of some of his notions."

"Maybe," sighed the mother.

All too soon Randy's visit had come to an end. He remained at the little farm over Sunday, going to church with his father and his mother, and left for the Hudson River early Monday morning.

Several days passed quietly and once more our hero fell into his routine work. Jones was sick, so the deckhands had a little more to do than usual. Randy pitched in with vigor, much to the satisfaction of Malloy and Captain Hadley.

One day, while handling baggage at the dock in New York, Randy was surprised to see Amos Bangs and a stranger come aboard. He soon lost sight of the pair and did not see them again until the middle of the afternoon, when he discovered them in a corner of the cabin, talking earnestly.

"It is queer Mr. Bangs should use this boat—

after his quarrel with Captain Hadley and Mr. Shalley," said our hero to himself.

He had occasion to pass the pair a little later and was surprised to hear the name of Mr. Bartlett mentioned.

"Don't worry; we'll down Bartlett easily enough," said the strange man, a fellow with bushy black whiskers.

"I hope so," answered Amos Bangs.

Curious to know what they could be saying about Jack's father, and remembering what he had heard in the past, Randy walked outside of the cabin and close to a window which was wide open. From this point he could hear what was said without being seen very readily.

"I don't like the way matters are standing," he heard Amos Bangs say. "We must make our position more secure, Tuller."

"I don't see how we are to do it," answered the man with the heavy whiskers.

"I wish I could get Bartlett to sell his stock and sign over all his interest."

"Can you do that without making him suspicious of what is going on?"

"Humph! He is suspicious already, that's the trouble."

"Does he know about the deal with Kastner?"

"I think not."

"It will be a blow, when he hears of it."

"I don't intend he shall hear of it just yet. If I had Robinson where I wanted him, I'd go ahead."

"Can't you get him?"

"Get him? I don't dare breathe a word to him." Amos Bangs laughed. "And the funny part of it is, Bartlett thinks Robinson is in with us."

"You are sure of that?"

"Dead certain."

"Then you must keep Bartlett and Robinson apart."

"If I can."

"What did you do with the papers you took from Bartlett's desk?"

"They are in my safe at home."

"Why don't you destroy them?"

"I will, some time."

"It is dangerous to leave them around."

"I am the only person who knows the combination of the house safe. The papers can't get out without me."

So the talk ran on for a good hour, during which time Randy heard many things which appeared to be of value to Mr. Philip Bartlett.

Then the two men arose and went to the smoking room, and that was the last our hero saw of them until they left the boat, half an hour later.

The talk he had heard set Randy to thinking. Plainly Amos Bangs and his companion were a pair of rascals and were trying to defraud Mr. Bartlett out of some if not all of his belongings.

"I'll have to call on Mr. Bartlett and tell him what I have heard," Randy told himself.

"See here!" called out Peter Polk, striding up as Randy was going to the lower deck. "What are you loafing around here for?"

"I am going below now," answered our hero.

"You can't shirk your work that way, Thompson." The purser came closer. "Listen," he whispered. "After this you keep your nose out of my business."

"I didn't know I had my nose in your business, Mr. Polk."

"Oh, you can't fool me, Thompson. I know it was you went to Captain Hadley with the story of how I was treating my relatives."

"You mean the Clares?"

"Of course I do. After this you keep your mouth shut," pursued the purser. "If you don't —well, you'll wish you had, that's all." And Peter Polk went away in extremely bad humor.

CHAPTER XXII

MR. BARTLETT MAKES A MOVE

As soon as the boat had tied up at Albany, and his work was at an end, Randy attired himself in his best and took a street car for the residence of the Bartletts. It was a humble place on a side street, quite in contrast to the fine residence the family had occupied in Riverport.

"Hullo, Randy!" cried Jack, as he came to the door to answer our hero's ring. "This is a surprise. Walk right in. Did you send word that you were coming?"

"I did not, Jack. Is your father home?"

"Yes, he is just finishing his supper."

"I want to see him."

"Had your supper?"

"Yes, I got a bite before I left the boat."

"All right—otherwise I know mother will welcome you at our table."

Jack went off to tell his father, and presently Mr. Bartlett walked in. He looked rather careworn and tired. Evidently his new situation was a hard one to fill and did not agree with him.

"How do you do, Randy?" said Mr. Bartlett. "Glad to see you. Jack says you want to see me."

"I do, Mr. Bartlett. Can I talk to you in private?"

"Certainly. Come into the parlor."

Mr. Bartlett led the way and closed the door. Then both sat down.

"I want to tell you something about Mr. Bangs and a man named Tuller," began Randy. "They were on the boat to-day and I overheard some of their talk."

"Tuller, eh?" said Mr. Bartlett, and his brow darkened.

As well as he could Randy repeated the talk he had heard. Jack's father listened with keen interest. He was astonished when Randy mentioned the papers which had been abstracted from his desk.

"So Bangs has them in his safe at home, eh?" he cried. "Well, I am going to get them, be the cost what it may. They belong to me, and I am going to take them no matter where I find them."

He was equally astonished to hear that a certain Mr. Robinson was not acting with Amos Bangs and certain other men, Tuller included.

"They gave me to understand that Robinson was with them," said Philip Bartlett. "If Robinson will only act with me, perhaps I can do a great deal."

"Then why don't you write to Mr. Robinson and find out?"

"I will go and see him."

"Oh, then he lives here."

"No, in Springfield. But our works are going to shut down for a few days, so I will have ample time. Randy, I am very thankful to you for bringing me this news."

"I hope it does you some good, Mr. Bartlett."

"I think it will. Perhaps I'll only be able to scare Bangs, but that may make him careful, so I can get something out of my stock in the iron works company."

"If you ever want me as a witness I will do what I can for you."

"Thank you, my lad; you are kind and I will remember what you say."

After that Mrs. Bartlett and Jack came in and learned something of what had brought our hero to the house.

"Good for you, Randy!" cried Jack. "Father, if I were you, I'd break into old Bangs's safe."

"Pray do nothing rash," pleaded Mrs. Bartlett. "Remember he is rich and has many friends."

"He is certainly rich," said Randy, "but I doubt if the family have many friends. All of them are too overbearing."

"Bangs broke into father's private desk and took the papers," went on Jack. "It would be only tit for tat to break open the safe and get the papers back."

"I shall see Robinson first and then make up my mind what to do," answered his father.

Randy spent a pleasant evening with Jack, and when it came time to go to the boat Jack walked half the distance with our hero.

"I wish father could get what is due him," said Jack on the way. "He can't stand the hard work he is now doing."

The next morning Randy sailed down the river on the steamboat. Twenty-four hours later Mr. Bartlett crossed the Hudson and took a train for Springfield. He hoped to find Mr. Robinson at one of the banks and he was not disappointed.

The bank official—for such Mr. Robinson was—listened with interest to all Philip Bartlett had to tell. He shook his head when Amos Bangs and Tuller were mentioned.

"I suspected as much," said he. "I was given

to understand that Bangs had bought you out. I couldn't understand it either, for you once told me that you did not wish to leave the works. I have just gotten back from a trip to Europe and have a good deal to attend to here, but I will take this matter up as soon as I possibly can."

"And you will stand in with me?" asked Mr. Bartlett, anxiously.

"If you wish it."

"I do."

"Then we must act together."

"And what would be your advice regarding those papers in Bangs's private safe at his house?"

"Get out a search warrant and take a professional safe man along, to open the strong box," answered the bank official, promptly. "And do not delay either. He may take it into his head to burn the papers up."

"I will do as you say," answered Mr. Bartlett with decision.

Some of his old-time will power had come back to him and he lost not a moment in carrying out his plans. He visited a firm dealing in safes and from them got the address of a man who claimed to be able to open any ordinary safe made. Then he called on this individual.

"You open safes?" he asked.

"I do—if I have the proper authority," answered the man.

"Can you open a first-class house safe?"

"Yes."

"How long will it take?"

"From five minutes to three hours."

"What are your charges?"

"Ten to fifty dollars. I'll have to see the safe before I can set a definite figure."

"Will you be at liberty to-morrow?"

"I'll be at your service if you engage me now."

"Very well, you may consider yourself engaged. I wish you to meet me in Riverport at about noon."

"Your own safe?"

"No."

"You'll have authority to open it?"

"I think so. I've got to go to court to get it, though."

"Ah! a legal case, eh?"

"Yes. You don't object, do you?"

"Oh, no, I have many legal cases. Had to force a safe for some lawyers in Bridgeport only last week."

"You will not disappoint me?"

"Not at all, Mr. Bartlett."

With this understanding Philip Bartlett left the safe opener and took a train back to his home. But, as it happened, a certain man saw him leaving the safe opener's office. This man was none other than Tuller, the friend to Amos Bangs.

"Bartlett, eh?" murmured Tuller to himself. "What is he doing in Springfield?"

He chanced to know the safe opener, whose name was Westinghouse, and presently dropped into the other's office as if by accident.

"How is business, Westinghouse?" he said, indifferently.

"Fair," was the answer. "Had two jobs last week."

"Good enough."

"How is business with you?"

"Booming. I suppose you get jobs ahead, is that it, or do you go out on the run, so to speak?"

"Sometimes I get orders ahead, but most of the jobs come in on the run—safe out of order, or something like that. I've got to go to Riverport to-morrow."

"Is that so? Bank?"

"No, a private party, I reckon. Going to have a safe opened by an order from the court, I think."

"Is that so! Well, I wish you luck on the job. Good-day."

"Good-day!" answered the safe opener.

Once on the street Tuller's face changed.

"Bartlett must have given that order, and if so he means to either open up the safe at the iron works or else the safe at Bangs's house. I must see Bangs and warn him, so that nothing is found which will do us harm!"

At first he thought to telegraph, but then came to the conclusion that it would be too risky. A letter might not be received in time.

"I'll go myself," he said, and an hour later was on his way to Riverport.

CHAPTER XXIII

THE PAPERS IN THE SAFE

At Riverport the next day Mr. Bartlett called upon a lawyer with whom he was well acquainted and told to the legal gentleman all that he had learned and proposed to do.

"I wish your assistance, Mr. Soper," he said.

"You shall have it," was the lawyer's prompt answer.

"Can you get an order from the court to open that safe?"

"I believe I can. Come, we will go and see the judge at once."

Fortunately for Mr. Bartlett the judge was easily found, and when the matter was explained he issued the necessary papers and placed them in the hands of one of the constables.

"But how are you going to open the safe if it is locked?" asked the judge. "Constable Carley is not equal to it."

"I have engaged a professional safe opener,"

answered Mr. Bartlett. "He can do the trick for the constable."

"Very well."

Mr. Bartlett, the lawyer, and the constable waited until the stage came in. The safe opener was one of the passengers and at once joined the crowd and was introduced.

In the meantime Jasper Tuller had also arrived in Riverport. In the morning he lost no time in calling at the iron works.

"I want to see Mr. Bangs," he said, to the clerk who came to wait on him.

"Sorry, sir, but Mr. Bangs went out of town late last night."

"When will he be back?"

"Not until some time this afternoon—possibly not until evening."

"Where did he go? I must communicate with him at once."

"He went to Rochester, but I can't give you the exact address," answered the clerk.

Jasper Tuller groaned in spirit. Could he have telegraphed to Amos Bangs he would have done so, but the telegram would have remained at the office awaiting a call.

"I must make a move on my own account, if I can," he muttered.

He called a carriage and was driven to the Bangs mansion. A servant answered his rather impatient ring at the front door.

"Is anybody at home?" he asked, abruptly.

"Mr. Bangs has gone away, sir."

"I know that," he snapped. "Is Mrs. Bangs at home?"

Now it happened Mrs. Bangs had come home the night before, intending to go away again two days later. But she had given orders that she wished to see no one.

"I—I don't know," said the servant girl. "I can see. What is the name?"

"Jasper Tuller. It is highly important that I see somebody of the family at once," went on the visitor.

Mrs. Bangs was in an upper hallway and overheard the talk. She knew her husband had had some trouble with a book agent over the payment of a bill and took Tuller to be that person.

"A gentleman to see you, Mrs. Bangs," said the maid. "He is very anxious about it."

"I cannot see anybody," returned the fashionable woman, coldly. "Tell him I am not at home."

The girl went down into the hallway, where she had left Jasper Tuller standing.

"Mrs. Bangs is not at home, sir. You will have to call some other time."

"Is Mr. Bangs's son at home?"

"No, sir; he is away for the summer."

"When will Mrs. Bangs be back?"

"I can't say, sir."

"It is too bad. The matter is very important. I came all the way from Springfield to see Mr. Bangs. They told me at the works he had gone to Rochester. I wanted to see him or his wife on business. Have you any idea where I can find Mrs. Bangs?"

The girl hesitated.

"N—no, sir," she faltered.

Mrs. Bangs was listening as before and now realized that something unusual was in the air. She slipped down a back stairs and out of a rear door. Then she came around to the front piazza just as the door opened to let Tuller out.

"Mamie, who is this?" she asked, looking at the servant girl meaningly.

"Are you Mrs. Bangs?" asked Jasper Tuller, quickly, and, as she nodded, he continued: "I am glad you have come. I am Jasper Tuller, one of the stockholders in the iron works. Perhaps you have heard your husband mention my name."

"I have, Mr. Tuller. What can I do for you?"

"I would like to see you in private"—this with a side glance at the servant girl.

"Very well, step into the library, Mr. Tuller," and the fashionable woman led the way to that apartment. Then the door was carefully closed.

"Something is wrong," said the servant girl to herself. "I wonder what it can be?"

She was of a decidedly inquisitive nature and not above playing the eavesdropper. She tiptoed her way to the library door and listened intently, while at the same time applying her eye to the keyhole.

"Now, what is it, Mr. Tuller?" asked Mrs. Bangs, after the door to the library was shut.

"Briefly, it is this," said the visitor. "Your husband has certain papers in his safe—papers which belong to another man,—Philip Bartlett."

"Proceed."

"I warned him to destroy the papers but he has not done so. Now Mr. Bartlett is going to come here, force open your safe, and take the papers away."

"Come here—force our safe!" gasped the fashionable woman. "He dare not do it."

"He is going to do it legally, I presume."

"You mean he will bring an officer of the law here?"

"Yes. If those papers are found it will look black for your husband, for he has no right to have them in his possession."

"Oh, Mr. Tuller, what shall I do?"

"It is easy enough. Open the safe, take out the papers, and put them where they cannot be found."

"Yes, but I do not know how to open the safe!"

"Don't you know the combination? Your husband said something about that, but I felt there must be some mistake."

"I did know the combination once, but I believe I have forgotten it," went on the fashionable woman. She knitted her brows. "Let me see. It was three 9's, I remember—9, 18, and 27."

"Yes! yes! And what else. See if you cannot think. It is so very important—not alone for your husband, but also for myself and others."

"I am trying to think. Let me see—yes, there was a 2 and a 3 and then another 2,—I mean so many times around."

"I believe I understand, Mrs. Bangs. You mean twice around to 9, three times around to 18, twice to 27, and then off at 0."

"Yes, yes, that is it!" burst out the lady of the mansion. "How clever some men are!" and she beamed on her visitor, who chanced to be well dressed and not bad-looking.

"If that is correct, I'll soon have the safe open," said Jasper Tuller, and walked over to where the strong box stood, in a corner of the apartment.

The lady of the mansion hovered near while Jasper Tuller got down on his knees and began to try the combination. He had to work the knob all of a dozen times before the door of the safe came open.

"At last!" he murmured, as the contents of the safe stood revealed.

"Do you see the papers, or rather, do you know them?" asked Mrs. Bangs.

"I will know them—if I can lay eyes on them," was the reply, as Tuller began to rummage around in the safe.

The papers were sorted out in different piles and he went through each pile as rapidly as possible. Presently he found what he wanted.

"Here they are!" he cried in triumph, as he held them up.

CHAPTER XXIV

ANOTHER HIDING PLACE

Mrs. Bangs breathed a sigh of relief when she saw the papers.

"You are certain you are right, Mr. Tuller?" she asked, anxiously.

"Yes."

"Where did those papers come from?"

"Mr. Bartlett's desk at the iron works."

"As they were in my husband's safe I think you ought to give them to me."

"I will do so, Mrs. Bangs. But you must put them where they cannot be found."

"Trust me for that."

"The officers of the law may search the whole house."

"Dare they do such a thing?"

"Yes, but if everything is found square your husband can sue Bartlett for damages," and Jasper Tuller chuckled loudly. "It will be a good joke on him."

"There are no more of the papers?"

"I will take another look and make sure."

This was done, but no more papers belonging to Philip Bartlett could be found. Then the safe was locked once more.

"I will put these papers away at once," said Mrs. Bangs and left the library with the documents in her hand. She was gone all of five minutes and came back smiling quietly to herself.

"Now they are safe," she said. "Nobody can possibly find them."

"I am glad to hear it," answered Tuller. "Now I had better be going—before Bartlett appears. Don't say anything about my having been here."

"I will not."

"And another thing, Mrs. Bangs. Pretend not to know how to open the safe. That will compel them to break it open, and your husband's case against Bartlett will be so much stronger."

"I shall follow your advice, Mr. Tuller. But look, somebody is coming already!" went on the fashionable woman, as a carriage turned in from the road and came toward the horse block.

"I must get out of this! Can I go by a back door?"

"To be sure," said Mrs. Bangs, and showed the way. As Tuller slipped out and passed toward the back road where Randy had had an encounter with Bob Bangs, there came a ring at the front door.

"Good-morning, Mrs. Bangs," said Mr. Bartlett. "Is your husband at home?"

"He is not," answered the fashionable woman, coldly.

"I've got a search warrant for this place," said the constable, pushing his way in, and he proceeded to read the document aloud.

"This is an outrage!" cried Mrs. Bangs, with assumed dignity. "An outrage, and you shall pay dearly for it, Mr. Bartlett. My husband is no thief, to steal your papers."

"Perhaps not," answered Philip Bartlett. "Nevertheless, I am going to have his safe searched and also this house."

"Well, since you have the law on your side, go ahead. But you shall answer to my husband for this indignity."

The constable began his work, and the safe opener approached the strong box and inspected it.

"Can you open it?" asked Mr. Bartlett, anxiously.

"With ease," was the answer. "This is one of the old-style safes."

"How much will it cost?"

"Ten dollars."

"Then go ahead."

The safe opener was soon at work. He turned the knob around slowly, listening intently in the meanwhile. He worked thus for perhaps ten minutes, when the door to the safe came open without an effort.

Mrs. Bangs was disappointed. She had expected that the safe would have to be blown open in the most approved burglar fashion, and was wondering what bill for damages she could render.

"You must have known the combination," she said, tartly, to the safe opener.

"This is my business," was the quiet answer.

The constable, with Mr. Bartlett's aid, went through all the papers in the safe. Of course the all-important documents were not found.

"Well?" asked the lawyer, after a long wait.

"They are not here," replied Mr. Bartlett. He felt sick at heart over his failure to bring the papers to light.

"Not here!"

"No, they must have been removed."

The library was searched, and then a look was taken through the whole house. Mrs. Bangs followed the men everywhere.

"You shall suffer for this outrage," she said to Mr. Bartlett several times.

"I presume I shall have to stand for what I have done," he answered, meekly. "Of one thing I am certain, Mrs. Bangs. Your husband has those papers, or else he has destroyed them."

"You can say what you please, Mr. Bangs is an honest man and a gentleman," retorted the fashionable woman.

At last there was nothing left to do but to leave the mansion, which Mr. Bartlett did with reluctance.

"I am afraid I have made a mess of it," he said to his lawyer. "I was certain we would find those papers."

"I am afraid you have hurt your case, Mr. Bartlett," answered the legal light, bluntly. "Bangs will now be on his guard and will take good care to keep those papers away from you."

"Perhaps he has destroyed them."

"That is not unlikely, since it would do him small good to keep them."

"What do you advise me to do next?"

"You had better wait and see what develops," said the lawyer.

The safe opener and the constable were paid off and Philip Bartlett returned to Albany in anything but a happy frame of mind. A day or two later he called upon Randy, when the steamboat tied up at the dock for the night.

"My fat is in the fire," he said to our hero, and told of his failure to locate the missing documents.

"Mr. Bartlett, I am sure Mr. Bangs said the papers were in his safe!" cried Randy. "He must have taken them out when he returned home."

"You can be a witness if the matter is brought into court?"

"Of course. I remember very well all I heard."

"Well, that is something," answered Philip Bartlett, hopefully.

He went home and the next day received a strong letter from Amos Bangs denouncing him for the action he had taken. Part of the letter ran as follows:

"I should sue you for damages, only I do not wish to drag you into court on account of your wife and family. In the future you need expect no favors from me. I am done with you. If you want to sell your stock in the iron company I will give you the market price, not a cent more. Remember, I shall be on my guard against you in the future, and if you dare to molest me again you shall take the consequences."

"He will do what he can to ruin us," said Mrs. Bartlett when her husband read the letter to her.

"I suppose so."

"What is the market price of the stock?"

"It has no regular market value now. Bangs will buy it for about ten cents on the dollar."

"Oh, Philip, that is so little!"

"I'll not sell the stock," said Mr. Bartlett. "I'd rather lose every cent than play into Amos Bangs's hands!"

CHAPTER XXV

A VICTORY FOR RANDY

ONE day Randy was out in Albany buying a new pair of shoes when he met Rose Clare, who was also doing some shopping for her mother.

"Oh, Randy, how do you do!" cried the girl, running up and shaking hands.

"Very well, Rose," he answered. "You look well."

"Oh, I am feeling splendid."

"It did you good to get out of New York."

"Indeed it did, and mamma is ever so much better too."

"I am glad to hear that. Do you like it at Captain Hadley's home?"

"Yes, mamma and Mrs. Hadley have become great friends."

"Do you go to school?"

"Yes. And, oh, I 'most forgot to tell you. I got a letter from New York to-day. It was from another girl, one who lived in the house with us.

She says Bill Hosker has come back to that neighborhood."

"To stay?"

"She says he is around every night."

"Then I am going to hunt him up."

"Oh, Randy, please don't get into any more trouble," pleaded Rose.

"He has got to give back my money, or take the consequences."

"You know what a ruffian he is!"

"I will be on my guard this time, Rose, and maybe I'll take a friend along," added our hero.

When he returned to the steamboat he told Jones about what he had heard. Jones was now feeling very well once again, and he readily volunteered to go with Randy and hunt up Hosker as soon as the boat got to the metropolis. Then Pat Malloy got wind of what was up and said he would go too.

"It's no use of going to the police wid such a mather," said the head deckhand. "We'll bring the rascal to terms ourselves."

It was a clear, cool night when the landing was made at New York. The deckhands hurried through their labors and then made off for the neighborhood where Randy had been attacked.

"Here is the spot where I was first robbed," said our hero, and pointed it out.

They walked around the neighborhood for nearly an hour, and were growing somewhat disheartened when Randy gave a cry:

"There he is!"

"You are sure?" asked Jones.

"Yes."

"Let me speak to him first. Then we'll know there ain't no mistake," went on Jones.

Randy was willing and he and Malloy dropped behind.

Bill Hosker had just come out of a saloon and was wiping off his mouth with the back of his hand. He turned down a side street.

"Hullo there, Bill Hosker!" cried Jones, pleasantly.

The bully and thief swung around on his heel and looked at the deckhand in perplexity.

"Who are you?" he asked, roughly.

"Am I right? Is this Bill Hosker?"

"Dat's my handle."

"Then you are the man I want to see," said Jones and beckoned for the others to come up.

When the street ruffian saw Randy his face changed color and he wanted to run away, but Jones grabbed him and so did Malloy. As both were powerful men, Hosker was as a kitten in their grasp.

"Youse fellers let me go!"

"I want you to give up the money you took from me," said Randy.

"I don't know you, young feller!"

"Yes, you do. Will you give up the money or not?"

"I ain't got no cash."

"Then you'll come to the station house with me."

"I bet yer I won't!" cried Bill Hosker.

He started to struggle when Jones hauled off and slapped him hard on the right ear.

"Now be good, or I'll shove a few of your teeth down your throat," said the deckhand. "This ain't no foolin' affair. Give up the boy's money and be quick about it. If you don't give up I'll maul you so your own mother won't know you!"

Bill Hosker was thoroughly alarmed. He did not mind going to the station house but he did mind a good drubbing, and he saw that those who held him were in no mood to be trifled with.

"Say, let us straighten dis t'ing out," said he at length.

"I want my money," answered Randy.

"Will yer drop de matter if I cough up de cash?"

"Yes."

"All right den. How much was it?"

"Four dollars and eighty cents."

The street ruffian pulled a small roll of bills from his pocket.

"Dare you are," he said, as he passed over five dollars. "Youse kin keep de change."

Randy took the bills and stowed them away in his pocket.

"I'll give the change to some poor person," he said. "I want only what is coming to me."

"Are ye done wid de rascal?" asked Malloy.

"Yes."

"Well, I'm not," answered the head deckhand.

"And neither am I," added Jones.

And then both hauled off and let Bill Hosker have it, right and left. The street ruffian had one eye blackened and a tooth knocked out, and went down in a heap more than dazed.

"Let that teach you a lesson," said Jones.

"It's better nor a month in jug," was Pat Malloy's comment. "The state won't have to feed the blackguard."

Randy had already walked on and his friends joined him, and all hurried back to the steamboat.

It was several minutes before Bill Hosker got up. "I'd like ter kill dem fellers!" he muttered.

He hurried for the nearest saloon, where he tried to drown his troubles in drink. In the saloon were several who knew him, and one man jeered him because of the black eye. This brought on another quarrel, and as a consequence both men were pushed out of the drinking resort. They continued to fight on the sidewalk, until a policeman came along and tried to stop them. Then Hosker attacked the officer, and as a consequence was placed under arrest. The next day he was brought up in court and sentenced to a year in prison for his misdeeds.

"I don't think he'll forget us," said Jones, as the steamboat was reached.

"Maybe he will lay for us," said Randy.

"Well, we can kape our eyes open," put in Pat Malloy.

"I shall not visit that neighborhood again," said our hero. "Now I have my money back I am satisfied."

"New York has altogether too many such toughs," put in Jones. "The police ought to clean them all out. When I first came here I was attacked in my boarding place on the Bowery."

"Were you robbed?"

"The fellow tried to rob me, but he didn't succeed. I played a neat trick on him."

"What did you do?"

"I had a roll of bills and these I placed in an inside pocket. I also had an imitation bank-bill —one of these advertisements you often see. Well, I took a small roll of paper and put the imitation bill around it, and put the roll in my vest pocket. The would-be thief got the roll and ran off with it."

"He must have been angry when he saw how he had been duped," laughed Randy.

"I didn't see that fellow again for nearly six months. Then I met him on the steamboat where I was working. When he saw me he sneaked out of sight in a hurry, I can tell you."

"Did you follow him up?"

"I tried to, but I didn't see him again until we were making a landing. Then I tried to grab him, but he slipped me in a crowd and went ashore as fast as his legs could carry him," concluded the deckhand.

CHAPTER XXVI

NEW TROUBLES

On the following day Randy noticed that Peter Polk seemed unusually sour and thoughtful.

"Something has gone wrong with him, that is certain," thought our hero. "I wonder what it can be?"

He did his best to keep out of the way of the purser and succeeded until nightfall. But then, when he was carrying an extra heavy trunk, Peter Polk got in his way and made him stumble and drop the piece of baggage. The trunk was split open at one end and some of the contents fell on the deck. It was a lady's trunk, filled with feminine wearing apparel, and a good many passengers laughed.

"What do you mean by running into me, you blockhead!" cried the purser, in a loud voice. "Why don't you look where you are going!"

"It was not my fault," answered Randy,

warmly, not liking the man's manner of address. "You made me drop that trunk."

"I did not. It was your own clumsiness."

"No, sir," said our hero, firmly; and a crowd began to collect.

"Don't dare to contradict me!" fumed the purser. "It was your fault, and the damage shall come out of your wages."

"Mr. Polk, it was not my fault and I shall not stand for the damage done."

"Ha! you defy me, eh, you cub! Go on about your work and I'll settle with you later."

"What is the trouble here?" asked Captain Hadley, coming up through the crowd.

"The blockhead of a boy dropped that trunk and broke it open."

"He ran into me and made me drop it," retorted our hero. He felt just reckless enough to stand up for his rights, be the consequences what they might.

"Put the trunk to one side, along with the other baggage," said the captain. "We have no time to waste on this just now. Get that other baggage ashore."

"My trunk!" shrieked the maiden lady, rushing forward. "Oh, who broke my trunk?"

"It was an accident, madam."

"And all my dresses spilt out, too! I shall sue the steamboat company for damages."

"We will settle with you, madam. I am sorry it happened," went on the captain, soothingly.

"It was a mean thing to do," said the maiden lady and began to weep. "Two of those dresses are brand-new."

"I guess they are not injured much."

Randy and the others had gone to work again. Our hero's thoughts were busy.

"I believe Polk ran into me on purpose," he whispered to Jones.

"Maybe he wants to get you discharged," answered the other deckhand.

"I don't see why."

"He's down on you because of that Clare affair."

"Do you think so?"

"Sure. He hated it worse than poison, for the captain now knows just how meanly he acted towards the widow."

The damaged trunk was passed over to a man on the dock and after some excited talk the maiden lady accepted ten dollars, with which to have the box repaired and her things put in proper order. It was more than was actually coming to her and she went off secretly pleased.

In the meantime one of the passengers, an elderly man who traveled on the line a great deal, went to Captain Hadley.

"What is it, Mr. DeLong?" asked the master of the vessel, kindly.

"I wish to speak to you about that trunk that was broken open."

"What of it?"

"I saw the accident. I was standing quite near at the time."

"Well?"

"I take an interest in that young deckhand of yours—he has done me several small favors from time to time. It was not his fault that the trunk was smashed, and I wanted you to know it."

"How did it happen?"

"Your purser got in the way and made the boy stumble. To me it looked as if the purser did it on purpose."

"This is interesting, Mr. DeLong. But I don't see why the purser should do such a thing."

"Neither do I, excepting he may have a grudge against the boy."

"Humph!" The captain grew thoughtful. "I will investigate this."

"Do so, and believe me, the boy is not to blame," said the elderly passenger, and withdrew.

As soon as the end of the trip came, and the work on deck was finished, Randy was called to the captain's office.

"Now what have you to say about that smashed trunk, Thompson?"

"I am not to blame, Captain Hadley," answered our hero, and told exactly how the incident had occurred.

"Do you mean to say Mr. Polk tripped you up?"

"He ran into me and made me drop the trunk. If I hadn't dropped the trunk I would have fallen down with the box on the top of me, and gotten hurt."

"This is a strange statement, Thompson. Why should Mr. Polk run into you?"

"He hates me, because through me your family learned how he had treated Mrs. Clare when he helped to settle her husband's affairs."

This threw a new light on the matter and the captain nodded slowly and thoughtfully.

"I did not think this of Mr. Polk."

"I think he hopes I'll lose my job," went on our hero. "He continually calls me a blockhead, just to get me mad. I think he'd like to see me lose my temper and pitch into him, and then he could get me my walking papers."

"I think I will have to put the damage to the trunk down to the regular expense account," said the captain at last. "In the future be more careful, and keep out of Mr. Polk's way."

"I will certainly be careful, and I'll watch him, too," answered Randy.

Evidently Peter Polk was surprised to see our hero go to his work whistling after his interview with the captain. He went to the master of the vessel himself a little later.

"Is that boy going to pay for the trunk?" he asked, sourly.

"No, you can put it down to the regular expense account," answered Captain Hadley.

"Humph! It was his fault."

"He says not."

"Did he blame it on me?"

"He did."

"It was his own fault."

"We won't argue the matter, Mr. Polk. Put it down to the regular expenses and let it go at that," and Captain Hadley turned again to the magazine he had been reading.

"Sticking up for the boy," muttered the purser, as he walked away. "Well, I'll get that cub yet, see if I don't!"

A day passed and Randy stuck closely to his

duties. He saw but little of Peter Polk and gave the purser a wide berth. The purser watched the youth narrowly, but said nothing.

"He has got it in for you," said Jones to Randy. "Take my advice and keep your eyes open."

"I am watching him."

"He is a man I shouldn't trust nohow. He has got a bad pair of eyes. I don't see how Mr. Shalley trusts him with all the boat's money matters."

"Neither do I," answered our hero.

"He could walk off with thousands of dollars if he wanted to," said Jones, and there the talk was dropped.

CHAPTER XXVII

RANDY MAKES A DISCOVERY

THE next day Randy wanted to change some of his underwear and went into his locker for his things. To his surprise he found in the locker a lot of wearing apparel that did not belong to him.

"Hullo, what does this mean?" he asked himself but could not answer the question.

He looked the articles over and made sure they did not belong to any of the other deckhands. Then as he was folding up an extra-fine outing shirt, he saw a letter drop to the floor. He picked it up and saw that it was addressed to Peter Polk.

"Can these things belong to Polk?" he asked himself. "If so, how did they get here?"

Curiosity prompted him to look into the envelope in his hand. Inside was a single sheet of paper on which was scrawled in a bold, heavy hand this brief communication:

"Peter Polk: If you don't pay me that commission of twenty dollars at once, I will go to old man Shalley and let him know how you are boosting up the expense account. G. A. G."

Randy read the letter with great interest. It was postmarked New York and the date was four days back.

"There is some mystery here," he reasoned. "What can it mean? Can Mr. Polk be cheating Mr. Shalley in some way?"

Then he remembered how the purser purchased all the supplies for the steamboat and paid the bills, and gave a low whistle.

"I must see Captain Hadley about this, and at once," he thought. "But no, maybe it would be better to go and see Mr. Shalley direct."

He placed the letter in a safe place and then went out on deck. He had just started to look for Captain Hadley,—to tell him about the strange wearing apparel—when Peter Polk rushed up to him.

"Look here, Thompson, I want you!" shouted the purser, wrathfully.

"What is it, Mr. Polk?"

"I've got you, you young thief!"

"I am no thief," answered our hero, warmly.

"You are!"

"Who says Randy is a thafe?" demanded Pat Malloy.

"I do."

"And I say it is false?"

"He has stolen some of my underwear," went on the purser. "Tell me what you have done with the stuff at once!"

"Your stuff is in my locker, Mr. Polk, but I did not take it."

"Ha! what a yarn to tell. Hand the stuff over at once!"

"You can get it if you wish," answered Randy, with a shrug of his shoulders.

"I will. Malloy, come along as a witness," answered the purser.

He walked to the compartment where the deck-hands slept and from our hero's locker hauled the articles that belonged to him.

"What do you say to that?" he cried, turning to our hero.

"I did not put the things there, Mr. Polk."

"If you didn't, who did?" sneered the purser.

"Perhaps you did yourself."

"Me!"

"Yes."

"You are crazy, boy! Why should I do such a thing?"

"To get me into troble. You hate me and want to injure me, that's why."

"Nonsense. You stole these things, it is useless for you to deny it."

"But I do deny it. I am no more a thief than you are—maybe not as much of a one," added Randy, significantly.

At these words the purser turned pale for a moment. But he quickly recovered.

"I shall report this to the captain."

"I'll report too."

"I'll have you discharged."

"We'll see about that."

Taking his things, Peter Polk went to the captain's office and told his story. Captain Hadley at once sent for Randy.

"This is a queer happening, Thompson," he said.

"Captain Hadley, I am not guilty," answered Randy. "It is only another plot of Mr. Polk to get me into trouble."

"And you think he put the things there himself?"

"I certainly do. I wish you would give me a day off," went on our hero, after an awkward pause.

"What for?"

"I wish to see Mr. Shalley."

"He is in New York, on business."

"So much the better. I can call on him there, after we tie up."

"Do you want to take this matter to him?"

"Not this alone. I have something else of importance. I know he will want to see me."

"Well, you can go. I hope you are not going to run away," and the captain smiled faintly.

"I have nothing to run away for, sir. Mr. Polk is down on me and I am going to do what I can to show him up, that is all. But please don't let him know that I am going to see Mr. Shalley."

"You have learned something important?"

"Yes, sir."

"About the purser?"

"Yes, sir. But I can't speak of it just yet to you."

"Well, what about this clothing affair?"

"Won't you let it rest for a few days?"

"If you wish," answered Captain Hadley, and then he was called away to attend to some important duties.

Although Randy did not know it, Peter Polk was nearby and caught a good bit of the talk between our hero and the captain. His face grew deathly pale when he learned that Randy was going to see Mr. Shalley and about his own personal doings.

"What has that cub discovered now?" he asked himself. "What can he tell about my doings?"

He was so worried he could not attend to his work. He turned the matter over in his mind and suddenly remembered the threatening letter he had received. He had paid the claim, but what had he done with the communication? He searched everywhere for it, but without avail.

"Fool that I was, that I did not tear it up and throw it overboard," he muttered to himself. "If that boy has the letter it may lead to an investigation, and then——" He did not finish but clenched his hands in rage and fear.

He watched Randy narrowly, and after New York was reached saw our hero make preparations to go ashore. He did not know that Mr. Shalley was in the metropolis and could not comprehend Randy's move.

"Are you going ashore?" he asked of our hero, when he got the chance.

"I am."

"Where are you going?"

"Excuse me, Mr. Polk, but that is my private business."

"Did Captain Hadley say you could go?"

"He did."

"Well, come to my office a minute, I want to talk to you," went on the purser, in a lower tone.

"Very well," answered Randy, and followed the man to the office, which at this time was deserted.

"Thompson, I want to know what you found in your locker besides my clothing," said the purser, after he had made certain that no outsiders were around.

"I found a cigar holder and a match safe."

"And what else?"

"I must decline to answer that question."

At this blunt refusal the brow of the purser darkened.

"You won't tell me?"

"No."

"Did you find a—er—a letter?"

"Perhaps I did."

"I want you to give it up."

"I didn't say I found it."

"But you did find it. It is my property and you must give it to me."

To this Randy was silent.

"Do you hear me?"

"I am not deaf, Mr. Polk."

"I know what you want to do!" hissed the

purser. "You want to get me into trouble. But I'll not let you do it."

"Maybe you'll get yourself into trouble."

"Bah! I am not afraid of a boy, but——" He paused and his manner changed. "See here, Thompson, you are a poor boy, aren't you?"

"I admit it."

"Well, some extra money will come in handy, won't it?"

"What do you mean, Mr. Polk?"

"I'll give you—er—five dollars for that letter."

"I haven't said that I had it yet."

"But I know you have it. Come, what do you say?"

"I say, I am going about my business," answered Randy, and started for the doorway.

"Not yet!" cried the purser, wrathfully, and flung him back into a corner. "You'll settle with me first, even if I have to call a police officer!"

CHAPTER XXVIII

OUT OF A TIGHT CORNER

RANDY was surprised and dazed by the treatment he received at the hands of the enraged purser and for the moment knew not what to do. He rose slowly to his feet.

"Don't you do that again!" he cried, a dangerous glitter coming into his eyes.

"I will do it—unless you give up that letter."

"You shall never have the letter, Peter Polk."

"Ha! so you admit at last that you have it!"

"I do."

"Then hand it over or I will call an officer and have you locked up."

"Call the officer, if you dare," and our hero shrugged his shoulders.

"You stole more than the clothing and the letter," went on the purser, craftily. "You took fifty dollars in money."

"I took absolutely nothing, and you know it."

"Then you want me to call in the officer?"

"Do as you please," said Randy, recklessly.

Peter Polk was nonplused. He did not want to call an officer. Yet he wanted to get the precious letter.

"You will save yourself a lot of trouble by giving up that letter, Thompson," he said, in a more subdued tone.

"Well, I don't intend to give it up."

"If I have you arrested I can send you to state's prison for five or ten years."

"I will risk it."

"What do you intend to do with that letter?" said the purser.

"That is my affair."

"Going to Mr. Shalley, eh?"

"Perhaps."

"It won't do you any good."

Again Randy was silent. He had stepped close to the door. On the instant Peter Polk did the same.

"You are not going just yet," cried the purser, meaningly.

Randy looked through the little window of the office. He heard footsteps approaching.

"Hullo there, Jones!" he called out.

"What's wanted?" came from the other deckhand.

"Come to the office, please."

In a moment Jones appeared. He was carrying a bucket of water and a deck swab.

"Now open that door," said Randy to Peter Polk. "No more nonsense, please."

"You are not wanted here, Jones!" cried the purser, angrily.

"You are wanted," said Randy. "Open the door. I want to get out."

Jones set down his pail and pulled on the door. Seeing resistance would be useless, Peter Polk allowed the door to come open. At once Randy stepped out into the gangway.

"I'll explain this to you some other time!" he called to the other deckhand, and then ran off before Peter Polk could stop him.

"Where are ye goin'?" called out Malloy, as he crossed the gang-plank.

"I'm off on business," answered our hero, and then paused for a moment. "Tell Jones to keep an eye on Mr. Polk, will you, please? It is very important."

"I will," was the reply.

In a minute more Randy was hurrying up the street. He knew where Andrew Shalley was stopping and took a car to the location.

The place was a well-known hotel and in the

corridor he met the steamboat owner, just ready to go out.

"Oh, Mr. Shalley, I want to see you!" he cried.

"What is it, Randy?"

"It's quite a story and very important."

"Then come to my room," and the steamboat owner led the way to the elevator.

As soon as they were in the room our hero told his story in all of its details and then produced the letter he had found. Andrew Shalley listened closely to the story and pondered over the letter for some time.

"Randy, have you any idea who this person who signs himself G. A. G. can be?"

"I've been thinking that over, Mr. Shalley, and I have found out that there is a head clerk who works for Bann & Shadow, the wholesale grocers, whose name is George A. Gaffney. Gaffney used to come and see Polk once in a while."

"And we buy a great many things from Bann & Shadow," put in the steamboat owner.

"So we do."

"I will look this man Gaffney up at once."

With the steamboat owner to think was to act, and going below with our hero he consulted a directory and found that George A. Gaffney lived on West Twenty-sixth Street.

"I will call upon this fellow," said he. "You can go along."

They took a car on one of the avenues and got out at the corner of Twenty-sixth Street. They had to walk half a block. The neighborhood was not of the best, and Gaffney's residence proved to be a four-story apartment house. The man lived on the top floor with his wife and four small children.

George Gaffney was at home, sitting in his shirt sleeves by a front window, smoking a pipe. He was surprised to receive visitors at that hour.

"Is this Mr. George A. Gaffney?" questioned Andrew Shalley.

"That's my name."

"Are you a clerk for Bann & Shadow, the wholesale grocers?"

"I am."

"I would like to see you privately, Mr. Gaffney."

"Who are you?"

"I am Andrew Shalley, the owner of the steamboat *Helen Shalley*."

"Oh!"

George Gaffney was taken aback and showed it plainly. His wife had come to a back doorway and was looking at the visitors curiously.

"Step in, sir," said the clerk, in a husky voice. "Mary, I will see this gentleman alone," he went on to his wife, who at once retired, closing the door after her.

Andrew Shalley was a good judge of character and he saw that George Gaffney was a family man of fairly good qualities. He was extremely nervous.

"I think I can get him to confess easily enough —if he has anything to tell," thought the steamboat owner.

"Please be seated," said the clerk, and Mr. Shalley and Randy sat down. Then there was a slight pause.

"Mr. Gaffney, I am afraid I have an unpleasant duty to perform," began Andrew Shalley, in a cold, hard voice.

"Why—er—what do you mean?" stammered the clerk.

"I refer to your dealings with my purser, Peter Polk."

"I—er—I haven't had anything to do with him—that is—we had some little business, but——" The clerk was unable to go on.

"You sent him a threatening letter the other day."

"Me? Who says so?"

"I have the letter in my possession."

The clerk winced and the steamboat owner saw that the shot struck home.

"This affair is a very serious one—you know that as well as I do," continued Andrew Shalley. "The fact of the matter is, it is a state's prison offense."

The mention of prison had the desired effect. George Gaffney broke down completely.

"Oh, sir,—I—I didn't mean to do any wrong—Polk said it would be all right. He got me to go into it—it was all his doings. All I ever got out of it was thirty-five dollars and that I will pay back. Mr. Shalley, I—er—I hope you won't prosecute me, for the sake of my wife and children!" And the clerk wrung his hands in despair.

"Didn't you get any more than thirty-five dollars?"

"No, sir, not a cent more, I swear it. And Polk said that was due to me legally."

"If that is true, I will not prosecute you,—but on one condition."

"Name it."

"That you tell me everything you know about Peter Polk's doings."

"I will do it, Mr. Shalley."

CHAPTER XXIX

GEORGE GAFFNEY'S STATEMENT

"I CANNOT tell you all Peter Polk has done," said George Gaffney, on beginning his story, "but I can tell you all so far as it concerns his purchase of goods from Bann & Shadow."

"That will be enough," answered Andrew Shalley, and brought out a book and a pencil, to take notes.

"He came to our firm three years ago and began to purchase various goods for the *Helen Shalley*. At first he met all bills promptly and never asked for any rebate or commission. That lasted for about three months."

"He must have been feeling his way."

"He was. At the end of six months he made a claim of a rebate on a bill for a hundred and fifty dollars and we allowed him ten dollars. Then he got ten dollars more on another bill, and after that he claimed a rebate of ten per cent. on everything he bought of us."

"You have all those bills on your books?"

"We have."

"Good. Go on."

"He gradually got bolder and wanted me to aid him in getting a commission elsewhere on regular steamboat supplies. I was willing to make a little extra money and introduced him to the firm of Leeson & Bronette. Leeson is an easy-going man and he promised Polk a big commission on all goods purchased. Polk bought hundreds of dollars' worth of goods from them, and got, I am pretty sure, from fifteen to twenty per cent. on every bill paid."

"Oh, what a rascal!" murmured Randy.

"Then I introduced him to another man, Aaron Denman, and he got goods from that man too and got his commission—how much I do not know. For introducing him to Denman I was promised that commission of twenty dollars. I saw Polk was making money hand over fist, and when he did not pay me I got mad and wrote the letter."

"And you are sure you never got a cent more out of him than thirty-five dollars?"

"Not a cent. Once in a while he treated me to a dinner and twice he sent me a box of cigars, and that is all. To tell the honest truth, I did not press him very hard, for I did not believe in what he was doing. I want to be an honest man, and I was led into this thing almost before I knew it," continued George Gaffney.

After that he went into a great many more details, to which Andrew Shalley and Randy listened with interest.

"I can get the actual figures for you from our books," said the clerk.

"What does your firm say to this?" asked the steamboat owner.

"Oh, they wanted the business, so they simply shut their eyes and didn't say anything."

"But that was dishonest."

"True—but such things are done every day," and the clerk shrugged his shoulders.

"If Peter Polk has been getting ten to fifteen per cent. on all goods he has been buying for me he has robbed me of thousands of dollars," said Andrew Shalley.

"It will be a hard matter to prove some of the transactions, Mr. Shalley. I guess he knew how to cover up his footprints pretty well."

"Well, if I can only prove some of them it will be enough for my purpose," answered the steamboat owner.

Before he left that night he drew up a long document containing the main facts of the case, and had George Gaffney sign it and had Randy put his name down as a witness.

"What do you want me to do, Mr. Shalley?" asked our hero, after they had left the clerk's house.

"You can go back to the steamboat. I am going to hire a first-class private detective to investigate this matter thoroughly. When I expose Polk I want all the evidence on hand with which to convict him."

"He will want to know what I did."

"That is true." Andrew Shalley mused for a moment. "Randy, you mind your own business," he said suddenly and sharply. Then he began to chuckle. "Now you can go back and tell Polk that I told you to mind your own business."

"I will, sir," and our hero grinned broadly.

"I will also give you a line to Captain Hadley," pursued the steamboat owner. "That will help to keep you out of further trouble."

The letter was penned, and a few minutes later our hero was on his way back to the boat. Andrew Shalley went in another direction, to hunt up a detective to work on the case.

It must be confessed that Randy felt much lighter in heart. He now knew exactly what kind of a rascal Peter Polk was, and felt that the purser could no longer drag him into trouble.

"He will soon come to the end of his rope, and that will be the last of him," said our hero to himself.

When he arrived at the boat it was very late and everybody but the watchman had gone to bed. He turned in without awakening any of the others and slept soundly until morning.

Much to his surprise Peter Polk did not come near him that morning, and our hero was kept so busy at one thing and another that he had little time to think about the purser and his nefarious doings. As soon as he got the chance he delivered the letter Mr. Shalley had given him to Captain Hadley.

The captain read the communication in silence. Then he uttered a low whistle and looked at Randy thoughtfully.

"I've been suspecting this," he said. "Randy, I believe you are to keep mum for the present."

"Yes, sir."

"I doubt if he troubles you any more."

"I'll be glad of it."

"Well, get to work, and some time we'll see what we will see," answered the captain; and there the talk was dropped.

It was a windy and cloudy day, and a majority of the passengers were glad enough to remain in the cabin during the trip up the river. About noon it began to thunder and the sky grew very black.

"We are up against a storm now," said Jones to Randy. "We'll have to take in some of the bunting."

The order was issued, and Randy set to work, with the other deckhands, to strip the decks. Soon it was raining furiously and all of the deckhands got pretty wet. All of the passengers had gone inside, so the decks were practically deserted.

Randy was folding up some bunting when he heard a quick step behind him. Turning, he saw himself confronted by Peter Polk. The purser's face was dark and full of hatred.

"Now, Thompson, I want to know what you did last night," snarled the man.

"I went ashore," answered our hero, as coolly as he could.

"To see Mr. Shalley?"

"Yes, if you must know."

"And you gave him that letter?"

"I did."

"What did he say?"

"He told me to mind my own business."

"What!" For the instant Peter Polk's face took on a pleased look. "So he really told you that?"

"Yes."

"Humph! I reckon you didn't expect such a reception."

To this remark our hero made no reply.

"Is the old man going to investigate?" went on Peter Polk.

"You had better go and ask him."

"You answer my question, Thompson!"

"I have nothing more to say."

At this the purser grew furious. There were many occasions when his temper got the better of him and this was one of them. He suddenly grabbed Randy by the throat, bending him backward over the rail.

"You little cur!" he hissed. "You are trying to get the best of me! But you shan't do it!"

"Le—let go!" gasped Randy. He could hardly speak.

"I'll let go—when I am through with you. But first I——"

What further Peter Polk had to say was drowned out by a violent crash of thunder. Then came a perfect deluge of rain, driven over the decks by a wind that blew almost with hurricane force.

Randy struggled harder than ever, but the purser continued to hold him. Then the steamboat, caught by the blast, careened to one side, and in a twinkling the youth was over the rail. Peter Polk released his hold, and down went poor Randy, until, with a splash, he sank beneath the waters of the Hudson River.

CHAPTER XXX

A SWIM FOR LIFE

THE shock came so suddenly that for the moment poor Randy scarcely realized what was happening. He went down and down and swallowed not a little of the river water.

When he came up, blowing and spluttering, he could see but little around him. Fortunately, he had gone off to the rear of the steamboat, thus escaping the danger of being struck by a paddle-wheel. All was so dark and the rain was so thick he could not make out the shore line.

"I've got to swim for it," he reasoned and struck out bravely.

It was no easy matter to keep afloat with so much clothing on. He listened, thinking he might hear the steamboat, but the roaring of the wind and rain drowned out every other sound.

Presently came another flash of lightning and then he saw the boat far ahead of him. No one but Peter Polk had witnessed his fall from the deck and nobody appeared to be coming to his assistance.

He kept his head well above water and at the next flash of lightning caught a glimpse of one of the river banks. Without further hesitation he struck out in that direction.

It was a long and exhausting swim and poor Randy thought he would never reach the shore. The current carried him far down the river, to where there was a small cove, lined with rocks on one side and bushes and trees on the other. He caught at some of the bushes desperately and at last pulled himself to a place of temporary safety.

For the time being our hero did nothing but try to get back his breath and his strength. In a general way he had an idea that he was some distance below the town of Catskill. What to do next he hardly knew.

"The first thing to do is to get out of this storm, I suppose," he told himself. "But that won't do a great deal of good, since I can't get any wetter than I already am."

Feeling a little bit rested, he presently got up and walked around the edge of the cove. Then he began to climb the river bank proper. It was hard work, but soon he came out on a river roadway and saw at a distance a hotel and half a dozen fashionable cottages.

"This looks familiar," he told himself. "Well, I declare, that place yonder must be the house at which Bob Bangs and his mother are stopping!"

Back of the house was a big barn and further to the rear was another building, used as a summerhouse and a place where oars and other things for small boats might be stored.

The summer storm was now letting up a bit. It was still raining, but the thunder and lightning had ceased and the wind had gone down. To get out of the rain and rest, Randy took himself to the summerhouse.

He was busy emptying the water from his shoes, when he heard somebody utter an exclamation and turning saw Bob Bangs standing near, umbrella in hand. The rich youth was staring at him in astonishment.

"Where did you come from?" he demanded, as he entered the summerhouse.

"From the river."

"You look pretty wet."

"I have been in the water quite some time."

"Oh! Did you fall overboard from the steamboat?"

"I did."

"You must be pretty careless," went on Bob, with a sneer.

"I certainly didn't fall overboard because I wanted to," answered Randy as lightly as he could.

"Say, I understand you are trying to get my father into trouble," pursued the rich boy, throwing himself on a bench.

"Who told you that?"

"Never mind. You are hand-in-glove with the Bartlett crowd."

"Well, why shouldn't I be, Bob Bangs? Jack is my dearest friend."

"Humph! I shouldn't care for him for a friend."

"And he wouldn't pick you for a chum," added Jack, quickly.

"I consider myself better than Jack Bartlett."

To this our hero did not answer.

"My dad is going to make it hot for old Bartlett," went on Bob. "He is going to sue him for defamation of character."

"When?"

"Oh, before a great while. Bartlett had no right to search our house and break open the safe."

"He had the law on his side."

"No, he didn't. Just you wait till my dad brings suit. It will ruin the Bartletts."

"I hope not."

"How do you like being a steamboat deck-hand?" went on the rich youth, to change the subject.

"Very well."

"It must be a dirty job," and Bob Bangs tilted his nose in the air.

"It might be worse."

"When I leave school I am going to be a lawyer."

"I hope you make a success of it."

"I shall—I am going to be one of the greatest lawyers in this country," added the rich boy, boastfully.

"Are your folks here?"

"My mother is. Dad is at the iron works."

"They tell me he isn't doing very well there," said Randy.

"He is doing fine. He discharged some of the good-for-nothing hands, that's all. Bartlett used to hire a lot of sticks."

"I don't believe it. Mr. Bartlett knows his business."

"Humph!"

The rain was letting up and Randy prepared to

walk to Catskill. As wet as he was, he resolved not to ask any favor at the hands of Bob Banks.

"Going, eh?" said the rich youth.

"Yes."

"Humph!" murmured Bob Bangs, and that was all he said.

Despite the steady rain, Randy walked rapidly to the town—doing this that he might not take cold. Once at the town he hurried to the steamboat landing.

"Hullo, where did you come from?" exclaimed the dock master, who knew him well.

"From a bath," answered Randy with a laugh, and then said he had fallen overboard from the *Helen Shalley* just before the landing at Catskill was made.

"Nobody said anything about it," said the dock master.

"I guess they didn't know it," answered our hero.

"What are you going to do now?"

"Telegraph to Captain Hadley and then stay in town until the boat comes back to-morrow."

"Better get dried off first. You can come to my house if you wish. It is not far off."

"Thank you, Mr. Ball."

Randy's telegram was a short one. It ran as follows:

"Fell overboard. Am safe at Catskill. Join boat to-morrow."

The telegram sent, our hero went with Mr. Ball to the latter's house. Here he was loaned some dry clothing and Mrs. Ball treated him to a late but satisfying supper. After the meal was over, and as it was now clear, he decided to take a walk around the town before retiring. Had he known of what that walk was to reveal he would have been very much surprised.

CHAPTER XXXI

NEWS OF IMPORTANCE

As was natural, our hero drifted down to the long steamboat landing. While he was standing around, he saw a ferryboat coming across the river, filled with passengers from the railroad station on the opposite shore.

As the passengers alighted he recognized Amos Bangs in the crowd. The rich manufacturer looked around anxiously, and presently caught sight of Mrs. Bangs, who had come to meet him in a carriage. Randy slipped out of sight.

"Well?" demanded Amos Bangs, as soon as he and his wife were together.

"Oh, Amos!" the woman cried, and could not go on.

"Is that all you can say, Viola?" demanded the husband, harshly.

"I can do nothing with the girl."

"And she knows where the papers are?"

"She does."

"How did it happen?"

"When Mr. Tuller called upon me she played the eavesdropper. She saw us open the safe and take out the papers, and when I went and hid the papers she followed me."

"But you said you were sure nobody knew where the papers were."

"I thought so at the time, but I was mistaken."

"How did it come out?"

"The girl did not sweep and dust the parlor to suit me, and I took her to task about it. She threw down her broom and said she would take no words from me. Then I told her to pack her trunk and leave the house. She grew more impertinent than ever, and said she would go, but I would have to pay her her wages regularly anyway. I asked what she meant. Then she told me to go and look for the papers I had hidden."

"And they were gone?"

"Yes. I was so overcome I nearly fainted," and Mrs. Bangs's face showed her deep concern.

"What next?"

"I went back to the girl and told her she must give the papers up or I would have her arrested. She laughed in my face. Oh, Amos, think of that horrid creature doing that!"

"She knew she had you," growled the rich manufacturer. "What did you do then?"

"Why—I—broke down, I couldn't help it. I asked her what she wanted for the papers. She wouldn't tell, and I said I would give her five dollars. Then she laughed in my face again. I wanted to drive her from the house, but I didn't dare."

"Did she say what she was going to do?"

"At last she said she would make a bargain—think of it—a bargain with a servant girl! She wants me to pay her wages regularly and also twelve dollars a month for her board."

"Will she work for you?"

"No, indeed, she says she will go and live with her married sister."

"Humph! Let me see, her name is Jackson, isn't it?"

"Yes, Mamie Jackson. Her sister lives over in Oakdale."

"Did she go to Oakdale?"

"I suppose she did."

"She must have the papers with her."

"No, I think she hid them, for she said we wouldn't find the papers even if we searched her and her trunk."

"I will have to go to Oakdale and see her,"

said Amos Bangs, after a pause in which he rubbed his chin reflectively.

The rich manufacturer and his wife had withdrawn to a corner of the dock while talking. Randy had kept nearby, behind some boxes and barrels, and had heard every word that was spoken. That he was immensely interested goes without saying.

"On the track of Mr. Bartlett's papers at last," he told himself. "Now, what had I best do about it?"

His one thought was to outwit Amos Bangs, and with this in mind he left the dock and walked rapidly toward the telegraph office.

"I wish to send another telegram," said he as he drew the pad of forms toward him.

"Must be your night for sending messages," answered the clerk, by way of a joke.

"I want this rushed through—it is highly important."

"All right, hand it over."

Randy hardly knew what to say, but soon wrote down the following, addressed to Mr. Bartlett:

"Papers taken from Mrs. Bangs by Mamie Jackson, a servant, now at sister's in Oakdale.

Hurry if you want to get them. Address me at Catskill."

Having sent the message, there seemed nothing for Randy to do but to retire. This he did, and was awakened two hours later by a message from Mr. Bartlett, which was in these words:

"Coming down first morning train. Meet me at Catskill Station, Hudson River Railroad."

Having received this message Randy consulted a time table and found that the first Albany train would arrive at the station across the river at about seven o'clock. He arranged to be on hand, and then tried to go to sleep again. But the most he could do was to take a few fitful naps.

As soon as the train rolled in Philip Bartlett alighted. Randy rushed towards him.

"Are you going to Oakdale?" he asked, quickly.

"Do you think it worth while, Randy?"

"I do."

"Then I will go. You must come along."

"I will," answered our hero, and then Mr. Bartlett got back on the train and Randy followed him.

"I left word with Mr. Ball, so Captain Hadley won't worry about me," Randy explained when seated.

"Now tell me what this means?" asked Philip Bartlett, impatiently. "I have been on the anxious seat ever since I received your telegram."

"I want you to get in ahead of Mr. Bangs," said our hero, and then told all he had overheard.

"I will make that servant girl give me those papers," said Mr. Bartlett, with decision.

"Perhaps you can scare her just as Mr. Shalley scared a fellow who was aiding another man to rob him," answered our hero. "I will tell you about that another time. I am pledged not to say anything just at present."

CHAPTER XXXII

BROUGHT TO TERMS—CONCLUSION

THEY had to make one change of cars and then take a stage running to Oakdale, which was but a small village four miles from Riverport. When they arrived it was close on to midday.

Fortunately for them, one of the storekeepers of the village knew Mamie Jackson's married sister and also knew Mamie, and he told them where to go. It was a dilapidated cottage on the outskirts, surrounded by a garden filled mostly with weeds.

"Not very thrifty people, that is certain," was Mr. Bartlett's comment.

"I think I shall know the servant if I see her," said Randy.

They paused at the gate and saw the two sisters near the side porch. One was on a bench shelling peas and the other was lolling in a hammock. Each looked very untidy and both wore wrappers that were full of holes.

"That is the servant," said Randy, pointing to the person in the hammock. "And see, she has some papers in her hands!"

"Step behind the wellhouse," said Mr. Bartlett, and this both of them quickly did.

"Well, go ahead and read the papers, Mamie," said the woman on the bench.

"Ain't no use, Sarah, I can't make head nor tail of 'em," answered Mamie Jackson.

"What do you suppose makes 'em so valuable?"

"I don't know. But I do know the Bangses don't want that Mr. Bartlett to get hold of 'em."

"I think you made a good bargain with the Bangses—that is, if they pay up."

"I'll make 'em pay. Oh, Mrs. Bangs was scart, I could see it." Mamie Jackson laughed shrilly. "And to think she was going to discharge me!"

"Well, I guess you gave her a piece of your mind."

"So I did. She is too stuck-up to live," went on the former servant girl. "When I get my money I'm going to have a fine dress too—and I'll buy you one, Sarah."

"Oh, Mamie, will you? I want a blue silk so!"

"I'm going to have a green silk, and a parasol to match, and then—Oh, dear! look at them bees!" And with a shriek Mamie Jackson threw up her arms and sprang out of the hammock.

For the moment the papers were forgotten, and quick to take advantage of the situation, Randy darted forward and secured them. Then he turned the documents over to Philip Bartlett.

"Who are you?" demanded the woman of the cottage, rising in alarm.

"It's that Mr. Bartlett himself!" shrieked Mamie Jackson, forgetting all about the two bees that had disturbed her, and which had now flown away. "Oh, how did you get here?" she faltered,

"I came after my papers—and I got them sooner than I anticipated," answered Mr. Bartlett, and there was a tone of triumph in his voice.

"Are those your papers?" asked the girl, trying to appear innocent.

"You know they are."

"I do not. I—I found them."

"I know better. You took them from where Mrs. Bangs hid them."

"Well, she didn't have any right to them."

"I know that well enough."

"I—I was going to send them to you," faltered the girl. She scarcely knew what to say.

"Really," returned Philip Bartlett, dryly. "Well, I will save you the trouble."

"It's a shame to suspect an innocent girl like me," said Mamie Jackson, bursting into tears.

"My sister never did anything wrong," put in the other woman.

"As I have my papers I won't argue with you," returned Mr. Bartlett. "But when the proper time comes you may have to explain how you happened to get the papers."

"Are you going to haul Mr. Bangs into court?"

"Perhaps."

"Well, I will tell what I know about them, if it will do any good. Mrs. Bangs and a man named Tuller plotted to keep the papers out of your reach. They opened the safe and took the papers out just before you came with that constable."

After that Mamie Jackson seemed anxious enough to confess and told her whole story, omitting to state how she had asked Mrs. Bangs to pay so much a month to her for keeping silent.

"We may as well go back to the town, and take the stage for Riverport," said Mr. Bartlett to Randy. "I will then telegraph to Mr. Robinson to come on, and we will settle with Bangs, Tuller & Company in short order."

"Will you make him give up the control of the iron company?"

"Either that or have him arrested for fraud."

The journey to Riverport was quickly made, and the telegram sent to Mr. Robinson. The bank official sent word back that he would be on in the morning. Then Mr. Bartlett went to a hotel and Randy hurried home.

"Why, Randy, is it really you!" cried his mother as she kissed him. "This is certainly a surprise."

"I didn't expect to come home," said he. "How are you and how is father?"

"I am real well as you see, and your father is doing splendidly. He says he feels better now than for three years back."

"That is good news."

"But what brings you?"

"I will tell you," said Randy, and sitting down he told his story, just as I have related it here. In the midst of the recital Mr. Thompson came in, and he listened also to what our hero had to say.

"I hope Mr. Bartlett gets what is coming to him," said Mr. Thompson. "And I hope Mr. Shalley brings that Peter Polk to terms also."

The next morning Randy received word to come to the iron works. He went and there witnessed a stormy meeting between Amos Bangs on one side and Mr. Bartlett and Mr. Robinson on the other. Randy was called in as a witness, and what he had to say made Amos Bangs gasp for breath and sink into a chair.

"You are going to expose me—to ruin me!" gasped Amos Bangs, at last, addressing the two men who had accused him.

"We shall expose you unless you give up the control here and do as we think is fair," said Philip Bartlett. "As for ruining you, I think you have about ruined yourself."

"But my wife, and my son——"

"Mrs. Bangs does not deserve my sympathy after what she has done. As for your son, he can go to work, as my son has done."

"Bob! What can he do?"

"Work may make a man of him. He will never amount to anything if you bring him up in idleness."

"It is hard!" groaned Amos Bangs. "I—I shall have to go to work myself!"

"That is what I was forced to do," answered Philip Bartlett, dryly. "But you will not be so badly off, Mr. Bangs. Your stock is worth at least four or five thousand dollars."

"Humph! That is not much. Well, I suppose I am cornered and must do as you say," and he gave a deep sigh. Secretly, however, he was glad to escape arrest.

A lawyer was called in, and the best part of the day was spent in drawing up and signing various legal documents. The iron works were thereby placed in the control of Mr. Bartlett, Mr. Robinson, and a stockholder named Wells, and Philip Bartlett was made the general manager of the company. All of the books and accounts were placed in charge of an expert accountant, and in the end Amos Bangs had to make good a deficiency of cash. The former rich man had to give up his elegant mansion, and soon after he and his family moved to the West without leaving their new address behind them.

When Randy went back to the steamboat, two days later, a surprise awaited him. An accountant, assisted by a detective, had gone over Peter Polk's affairs and discovered that the purser had robbed Andrew Shalley of between eight and ten thousand dollars. Polk had taken time by the forelock and fled. He tried to get to Canada, but telegrams were sent out, and he was caught just as he was trying to cross the Suspension Bridge at Niagara Falls. Later on he was brought back and tried, and received three years in prison for his crimes. He had nearly six thousand dollars of the stolen money in the bank, and this was turned over to Andrew Shalley. Two hundred and fifty dollars went to Mrs. Clare as part of her husband's estate.

"Bringing Peter Polk to justice is due to you, Randy," said the steamboat owner, after the affair was a thing of the past. "I feel I must reward you for what you did."

"I don't ask any reward, Mr. Shalley. I am glad that I cleared my own name."

"Here is something for you, nevertheless," said Andrew Shalley, and handed a big document to our hero.

"What is it?"

"It is the deed to the farm on which your folks are living. It is made out in your name. I bought the place from Peter Thompson, your uncle. Now you have something that you can really call your own," and Mr. Shalley laughed pleasantly.

"Mr. Shalley, you are more than kind," cried Randy, warmly. "Do my parents know of this?"

"No. You can go home over Sunday and surprise them."

"I will, and I thank you very much, sir."

Randy went home, and there was a general rejoicing over the good news. But more was to follow.

"I met Mr. Bartlett to-day," said Mr. Thompson. "He says they want a first-class carpenter at the iron works to take charge of the repairs. He offered me the place at a dollar a day more than I am getting."

"Good enough, father!" cried Randy. "That is just like Mr. Bartlett."

"He said he wanted to do something for us on your account. And he sent you this," added Mr. Thompson, and brought out a neat silver watch and chain. It was a nice present and pleased Randy greatly.

Not long after that the season on the river closed and Randy came home for the winter. As his father now had a steady place at good wages, the youth went to school, in company with Jack Bartlett, who had moved back to Riverport with the rest of his family. Randy was a good scholar and made rapid progress.

"I want you to get a good education," wrote Andrew Shalley to our hero. "Then, later on, you can enter my office if you wish, or take a better place on the steamboat."

Six years have passed since that time and Randy has finished his education. He is now the general manager for the steamboat company, and rumor has it that he is soon to marry Rose Clare, who still lives with the Shalleys. He is prosperous, but come what may, will never forget the time when he was only a deckhand.

THE END